The Forgotten Guardians

The Forgotten Guardians

Rachel Hoffmann

Keep on Reading!

Rachel Hoffmann

ISBN 978-0-557-40689-0

This book is dedicated to:
Mrs. Giersbach for introducing me to the world of
writing, Mr. Toth for correcting grammatical errors,
and my family and friends for encouraging me and
giving helpful advice

\

Chapter 1

Zora

I never really imagined my life as a fairy tale, but I am queen of the Land of Inspiration and am free to do as I wish. For the longest of times, I didn't think such a glorious land was real. I thought I had actually created it, but it turns out it had existed long before I was born, or so one of the butterflies of the land had once whispered as it fluttered past my ear.

The Land of Inspiration is a happy one, I realized, as I walked with bare feet on the soft lush grass. My dark green dress just brushes the ground slightly, and the silver crown on my blond, perfectly straight hair shimmers in the sunlight. A golden retriever named Lucky walks by my side, with a concerned look on his face. No collar marks his neck, for he is a free creature, but yet he follows me wherever I go.

I stopped and bended gracefully to stroke a rabbit that stopped at my feet. I caressed the rabbit's ears, for even though it hasn't said I word, I know what all the creatures wish of me. The rabbit quickly thanked me, and with a bound and a leap he is off again, exploring the vast land on which he lives. The Land of Inspiration is made up of rolling hills of grass and flowers and vast forests with many different kinds of trees. There are also rivers and waterfalls and canyons and mountains. All of the landforms are marked with a certain beauty that can only be found in the Land of Inspiration.

As my eyes wandered over the land, Lucky opened his mouth and said, "Queen Zora, I sense you are not happy here. What troubles you?" Regret is in his voice, as if the sadness in me is because of him.

I looked down at him and smiled as I said, "I don't quite know what you're talking about, my friend. How could anyone possibly be sad in a land with no worries? This is like heaven on earth. There is endless fruit and plentiful water, so I need not fear of going hungry or dying of thirst. I am the queen and as far as I'm concerned, everyone respects and loves me and I, in return, love this land and its inhabitants."

Lucky pondered what I had said, but replied quietly, "But Queen Zora, there are no humans here. I took you away from your home to save it and the Land of Inspiration, but now I fear you are lonely inside. Queen Zora, I can send you back if you miss your friends and family. I'm not quite sure how yet, but I'm sure there's a way."

I was not quite sure what Lucky was talking about, so I inquired, "What friends and family? My friends and family are the creatures of this land. I am the only human, but that does not trouble me. There's a difference between being alone and being lonely. I'd say I'm alone, but not lonely."

Lucky was quiet for a long time and he averted his gaze away from me. When he looked back up I saw that he was crying. I was puzzled, but before I could say anything, Lucky murmured, "Oh Zora, I am sorry I did this to you. Have you truly forgotten what happened? Remember, there was that boy that you loved? You said you would do anything for him, and so you have, but I took you away from him before you could even have a chance at true love. The Land of Inspiration needed you though, so I had no other choice. Don't you remember?"

I shook my head, and so he sighed and said, "I should tell you then what happened, but I'm afraid you would get lonely then and hate me if I did."

I walked a little ways towards an apple tree and plucked one of the fruits. Another one quickly grew in its place. Lucky had followed me and I said, "So then don't tell me. What would it matter?"

I took a bite from the apple as Lucky replied, "Your heart, Zora … there's a piece missing. I hate seeing it gone, for it was one of the pieces that always amused me the most. If I can send you back, I think it can be restored."

I shrugged and then stated, "I'm still not sure what you're talking about. I don't feel anything missing. I still love, so it must not be that part of my heart that I'm missing. I feel normal."

Lucky remained quiet as a purple unicorn with a white mane and tail approached us. I smiled warmly at her as I said, "Hey Emily, how are you this fine day?"

The unicorn, Emily, replied happily, "I am well, thank you. And how goes your health, Queen Zora?"

I nodded politely at her and said, "I am well." There is silence, and I add, "Though Lucky thinks I am lonely. Do you think I'm lonely, Emily?"

Emily glanced at Lucky and me in confusion, but then walked up to me and rested her horn on my shoulder. Her horn glowed many colors, and when she pulled away, the horn stopped glowing and returned to its crystal like form. She shook her head and said, "I don't feel loneliness inside of you … only happiness and good health, like you said. Perhaps I should get one of my other friends to—"

I cut her off, "No, I am fine. I trust that what you say is true, for I do not feel lonely either. If you say I am not lonely, then I must not be."

Emily nodded and plucked an apple from the tree. As before, another one quickly grew in its place. As Emily crunched on the apple, Lucky stared at her and asked, "How can you be certain Zora is one hundred percent happy? Can't you see that a piece of her heart is missing? Surely she can't be entirely happy if a piece of her heart is missing."

Emily glared at Lucky and retorted, "*Queen* Zora isn't missing anything. Can't you let it go Lucky? Can't you see that Queen Zora belongs here with us? She is better than those other humans. With them her talents would be wasted. She saved our home from doom, don't you remember?"

Lucky grew somber as he responded, "Emily, you know just as well as I do that her talents wouldn't go unrewarded in her world. She could become a famous author or artist. Besides, I think she belongs with her people. Don't you remember that boy that she loved?"

Emily snorted, "You mean the boy that didn't realize what a treasure she was until it was too late? He had his chance with her and he blew it. Queen Zora is happy with us now, and it's just as well that she doesn't remember him. He made her heart ache too much, and it distracted her from her talents."

Lucky looked at me and then back at Emily and murmured, "I think it made her want to achieve more for him, so I think it made her talents improve."

Emily shook her head and said, "Well it doesn't matter, either way. There's no way to send her back, and besides, she doesn't even remember her old life. It would be torture sending her back to a world that is not as carefree as this one. And don't you try and get her to remember her old life, especially if you don't know how to send her back."

The conversation between Emily and Lucky could have very well been in a different language. I knew they were talking about me, but I didn't know what about. What of a different world with people? I laughed at such a crazy idea. I was the only human in this world. There's no other land besides this one. There was the Sea of Interference, but that was different and didn't affect the Land of Inspiration. So I was told anyways.

Emily said farewell to Lucky and me and then trotted off towards a nearby forest. I on the other hand, continued to walk across the meadow towards the only building that existed in the land. It was a grand castle, made of white marble. Inside were many rooms, but I rarely was inside. I spent a lot of my time outside, exploring the land, for there was always something new to see. It was impossible to be bored.

As I trudged across the bridge and through the door that was always open, a bluebird flew past me and chirped a quick good morning. I waved to it and said good morning as well and then it flew away. I stood still a moment, watching it fly and commented, "Isn't it wonderful, Lucky?"

Lucky looked at me, perplexed, and asked, "Isn't what wonderful, Zora?"

I gestured towards where the bluebird had flown and replied, "Wings and flying. I would love to have a pair of wings of my own. Wouldn't that just be wonderful?"

Lucky shook his head and responded, "I don't know … I prefer the ground myself, but if it pleases you, I could call in a flying creature and you could go flying with them on their back. You can have everything here ... well, except for one thing."

I continued to walk in the castle and Lucky followed me. I entered into a large hallway and saw many doors on both sides of me and a large staircase in front of me. I headed up the marble staircase and into a large bathroom. The large white tub had golden polished handles, and the toilet was a matching white and gold. Lucky stopped outside the door and asked, "Queen Zora, aren't you curious as to what you can't have here?"

I shook my head and closed the door on him. I heard him whimper on the other side, but then he pattered away. I knew he would be there when I got done taking my bath, so I took as long as I could. I stripped myself of my clothes, and placed my crown on the marble sink counter that was in the bathroom. I turned the water faucet on and in seconds the tub was completely full of warm water—not too hot and not too cold. The bathtub was of magical sorts and filled within three seconds of perfect-temperature, soapy water. As I climbed into the tub and submerged myself into the water, my clothes that I had taken off suddenly vanished and new clothes appeared on the marble sink counter next to my crown.

As I sat soaking in the water, I closed my eyes lightly and let my thoughts drift lazily about. There really wasn't much to ruling this land. The creatures took care of themselves quite well. The more I lay in the tub soaking and thinking about this fact, a sudden sense of curiosity began to envelop me, and I found myself wondering why I was made queen. I decided I wanted to know right then and there why, and I knew that Lucky would be able to tell me. I probably had asked him the question before, but in this land that I ruled, I asked so many questions, I sometimes forgot the answers to them.

I quickly got out of the tub, and a towel suddenly appeared in the air. I grabbed it and dried off, and then got changed into my new clothes. I put my undergarments on first, of course, and then slid the aqua blue dress over my head. A brush appeared in front of me, just as the towel had, and I grabbed it and ran it through my silky hair. When I was done, I put it on the counter, and it vanished. Lastly, I placed the crown upon my head, and then opened the door. As I had predicted, Lucky was sitting on the top of the stairs and looking at the door I had just opened. When he saw me, he smiled uncertainly and asked, "How was your bath, Queen Zora?"

"Good," I replied, "But I came out earlier than I would've wished because a question was bothering my conscience."

"And what would that be, my friend?"

I hesitated, but he remained sitting, waiting for my question. Finally, after many seconds, I asked, "Why was I made queen? I don't really do much ruling. This land is all happiness. It's almost as if there's a power that makes all creatures here peaceful and agreeable."

Lucky nodded and said, "Of course there is a power here that does that, and that power comes from you. You are a rare child, Zora. That's why I had to take you here. Before you came here, chaos from the Sea of Interference was troubling this land, but now all is right."

I pondered this and then stated, "I still don't understand half the things you're saying. I've lived here all my life. What do you mean by 'taking me here'? And I thought the Sea of Interference doesn't affect our land."

Lucky was quiet for a while before he replied quietly, "The Sea of Interference doesn't affect our land … anymore that is. Its power has only left us because you came. We needed you to ward off its power because once it took over our land it would've affected the land where you originally came from. Don't you remember, Zora? Don't you remember any of your past life?"

"I assume I've lived here and ruled this land all my life; that's all I remember if that's what you're asking. Lucky, I don't know where you get such crazy stories. Me coming from somewhere else—that's silly."

Lucky sighed, exasperated, but he followed me down the staircase just the same and asked, "So what do you want to do now, Zora?"

I walked out of the castle and another bird flitted by. This time it was a cardinal. I pointed at it and answered, "I think I would like to fly. Can I fly, Lucky?"

Lucky nodded and said, "A dragon makes a wonderful steed for the air."

I looked up in the sky toward where Lucky had suddenly barked, and saw a magnificent silver dragon. The dragon circled overhead a few times as it slowly descended towards us. When it landed, the ground shook and a great wind blew about us.

The great dragon had ebony nails and sharp green eyes. The spikes on his silver back were gold, and he sparkled like a diamond in the afternoon sun. The dragon bent his head towards me and said in a deep voice, "Good afternoon my queen. I hear you would like to fly, and I am offering you a ride on my back."

I smiled warmly at him and answered, "Thank you most magnificent beast. I would love to fly with you. Where do you suggest I sit?"

The dragon lifted his front paw and pointed to his back where there was a large gap between two of his spikes. It was near the lower part of his sleek neck. I climbed on his back and put my arms around his neck, but the dragon laughed lightly and said, "My queen, do not hold so tightly, I will not let you fall. You will choke me if you hold so tightly."

I loosened my grip a little bit, and I felt the dragon crouch low before he pushed up with his mighty limbs. He flapped his wings a few times to gain elevation, and then many more times to climb higher into the sky. Lucky followed the dragon's shadow from below, and as he did so I thought to myself, *what a silly dog, loyal, but silly.*

When the dragon seemed satisfied with its height, it seemed to just glide in the air a little bit so I could look at my surroundings and enjoy my height. After a while I asked, "Mighty dragon, what is your name?"

The dragon replied, "Conrad Silverscales, but you can just call me Conrad."

"Conrad," I murmured quietly to myself, and then I said louder, addressing the dragon beneath me, "Conrad? If it's not too much to ask, could you maybe fly a little faster?"

Conrad turned his head and flashed a toothy grin as he replied, "Of course, Queen Zora, but now you'll want to hold on tight. Here we go!"

With that, Conrad quickly flapped his wings and began to plummet towards the ground with all the speed he could muster. I felt my stomach lurch, but with a pleasurable feeling as we soared through the air. Just as I thought the dragon would hit the ground, he pulled up sharply and climbed upwards again towards the sky. He flew in loops and turns and twists. Much of it was fancy stuff, or so he told me later, but all of it was thrilling for me.

After a while, he slowed down and, panting, he asked, "Would you like to fly more Queen Zora?"

I quickly replied, "No, I am fine. Conrad, I didn't mean for you to wear yourself out like that. Now you must rest, for surely you are very tired. Take me back down to Lucky please, and then you can go."

Conrad replied with a bit of dignity, "I am not tired Queen Zora. The sun gives me all my energy. I am just panting because flying makes me excited—it was just so exhilarating! But if you wish, I will take you back down."

He turned to look at me and I nodded as I apologized, "I'm sorry Conrad—I didn't mean to offend you."

Conrad shrugged it off and then flew me back to the ground. When he had flown away and I was rejoined by Lucky, I said, "That was fun, Lucky … absolutely breathtaking. You should have joined me."

Lucky shook his head and replied, "Nay, like I've told you before, I prefer to stay on the ground. I'm a dog, not a beast of the air." Lucky paused and then asked, "Now what will you do?"

I thought a while and then for some reason unknown to me, I remembered Lucky saying that I could have anything in this land except for one thing. I know before I told him I wasn't curious, but all of a sudden I was. I stared at Lucky for a long while and then asked, "Lucky, what is the one thing that I cannot have in the Land of Inspiration?"

Lucky responded quite quickly, "That's true love of course. I told you that the day you agreed to come here. Don't you remember?"

I shook my head and stated, "Well, why would I care? True love—what is that, and why can't I have it?"

Lucky looked at me with mournful eyes and murmured, "You really don't know? How can you not know? You always yearned for true love in your other world. You came to this world and sacrificed any chance that you would have with that boy so that his world—your original world—wouldn't fall to pieces. Anyway, you can't have true love here because there are no people like you here."

I sat in silence, trying to figure out the meaning of Lucky's words, but to no avail. Lucky whispered to me, "That's the part of your heart that's missing, Zora. I know you are capable of loving the creatures of this land, but your love and knowledge of your own kind has vanished. That was the sacrifice you made. Aw, Emily would kill me for telling you these things. She knows part of your heart is missing, but she won't admit to it because she's not your true friend. Zora, I was always with you. Do you remember me always being with you?"

I nodded and replied, "You've been following me around since …" I trailed off. Suddenly, I couldn't remember how long I had been ruling the Land of Inspiration.

Lucky caught me faltering and said, "Ah. You see? You are forgetting things. You don't know when or where we first met do you?"

A herd of deer suddenly sprang out of the forest closest to us. They ran across a vast meadow and Lucky and I watched them suddenly stop to graze and play. I smiled at their appearance and said, "This place is amazing Lucky. I never grow tired of living here, but as for what I'll do next, I'd think I would like to hear a story. Can you tell me a story?"

Lucky seemed annoyed that I had avoided his question, but I didn't know how to answer it, to be honest. He sighed and answered, "I can tell you a story. Sit down though and get comfortable, it will be a long one."

I obliged and sat down, but before Lucky started, I asked, "What story will you be telling Lucky?"

Lucky thought a moment and then replied, "How about I'll tell you a story about a girl, who was very much like you, and her best friend, a dog."

"That sounds good. Though it will be hard to imagine, for I've never seen other people before."

"Fine, I'll tell you our story then, since you seemed to have forgotten it. Will you listen to the whole thing though and try to remember?"

I promised I would, so Lucky began, "You were young, Zora, when we first met. I think you were about four when you thought of me and created me out of your imagination."

I interrupted him, "You mean I created you? Is that why you're always following me around, even though you're a free creature? What about the other creatures here, did I create them too? If so, how come I don't remember it?"

Lucky answered, "No, you only created me. I'm your best friend here Zora; that's why I follow you around. That's also why I don't feel obligated to call you Queen Zora or 'my lady' all the time like the other creatures. Any more questions, or may I continue?"

I waved my hand and said, "No, I'm good for now. You may continue."

Lucky nodded and said, "For a while, I was just your imaginary friend, but when I still remained with you in fifth grade, you were finally convinced that I was something more. I told you I was there to help with your talent—do you know what that talent is, Zora?"

I thought a moment and then guessed, "Keeping the peace?"

Lucky tilted his head and answered solemnly, "Well, I suppose you are capable of doing that, but I'm talking about your other talent— writing stories and drawing. It's your massive amount of creativity that had drawn me to you and inspired me to stay with you up until twelfth grade when …" Lucky faltered, but then continued on, "When it happened. When the Sea of Interference came to this land and required your unique gift to stop it from overwhelming the goodness. With you in this land, it was forced to go away and so you saved both worlds."

I interceded again and questioned, "What 'both worlds'? Lucky this is the only world that exists—well, besides the Sea of Interference, but why would that need saving?"

He shook his head and I saw a look of frustration on his face as he grumbled, "No, I mean your old world and this one. I don't consider the Sea of Interference a world. Zora, you promised you would try to remember. You need to stop denying the existence of your old world. If you remember you can retrieve the lost part of your heart."

I looked away from Lucky as I heard two bucks in the meadow ram into each other. They were just playing of course, but it amused me. Lucky was quiet while I watched, but I heard a low growl come from his throat, and when I looked back towards him, Emily was standing by him and glaring at him.

"Hi Emily, what are you doing here? Can I help you with anything?" I asked.

Emily gave Lucky a fierce look again before looking up at me and, softening her look, she replied, "Oh no, I was just wondering about the story Lucky was telling you. It seems very interesting, but fake. How can another world besides this one and the Sea of Interference exist?"

I was about to comment on it, but Lucky snarled, "Emily, you know another land exists, it's where Zora, oops sorry, *Queen* Zora came from. Emily, seeing this part of the heart missing in Queen Zora troubles me. Isn't there any way I can send her back? Don't you remember how much she yearned for true love?"

Emily pondered Lucky's words for a minute before she replied, "Maybe if she remembers her past life, but that's still not guaranteed to send her back. And what if she remembers and is enveloped with sadness because we *can't* send her back? Right now she is happy in this heaven-like world, so why are you trying to send her back? She chose to come here, remember? She chose what she did to save our world and *him.*"

Lucky murmured, "But deep inside the part of her heart that was set to cold black, she is sad. I sense it, for I am a part of her."

Emily was about to argue again, but I intervened, "Wait, Emily, I want to hear Lucky's story. He's a very good story teller, and I'm curious now. Besides, I probably won't remember what you don't want me to remember. I don't even know what you two are babbling about."

Lucky gave Emily an I-told-you-so look, and Emily sighed heavily. She turned her back on us, and before trotting away, she said, "Very well, you may continue on, Lucky."

I looked at Lucky expectantly and he returned my look with a thoughtful expression. Then he stated, "Wait a minute. I've got an idea; you'll see the story from my point of view. I can enter your mind if you'll allow me and you'll understand everything better, but I'll have to take breaks in between, I'm not sure how much this is going to tire me out. I'll start with when you first created me. Are you ready?"

I was confused with Lucky's idea, but I nodded anyways. I watched as he began to turn transparent and then float towards my head. Before he entered my head through my ears, he whispered gently, "Close your eyes and lay down. You are about to see your story from my point of view."

I was shrouded in darkness, and in a moment, my eyes were opened to be looking through the eyes of a dog. His thoughts echoed through my head and he told his story …

Chapter 2

Lucky

I was created from guardian airs sent to a four year old by the Dove of Light. The girl has straight blond hair and beautiful blue eyes. Her name is Zora, and I am her golden retriever, and she is my girl. She names me Lucky. Her mind is colorful and wonderful inspiration and stories lie in it. I tell her I am from the Land of Inspiration and she asks what that is. I send her pictures of it through her mind and she smiles when she says, "It sounds like heaven."

She is the only one who can see me, she says, but I know others can see me if I let them. I am *her* gift, however, and can not show myself to other humans unless the Dove of Light allows it. When she is young, I will act as her imaginary friend and help her creativity and imagination grow. When she grows older however, I will have to give her more proof that I exist and am not all just a figment of her imagination. I will act as a conscience. I will also encourage her to never give up her dreams, but for now I am content to be just a friend.

Zora tells me that her older brother, Bradley, has imaginary friends as well. She tells me they are robot-ghosts, and I tell her I can see them. But when I look into her brother's mind, I see it is not quite as colorful as Zora's and I know he will soon forget his friends. When I tell the robots this, they are not too upset, for they know he will forget them as well, but they say they will be his friend as long as he wishes them. They also tell me that even when Bradley forgets them, they will continue to watch over him from the Land of Inspiration, for that is what the life of a guardian from the Land of Inspiration is all about.

This life is something new for me; I know I will be Zora's best friend for as long as she lives, but I don't know what would happen to me if she ever forgot me. The robots are more knowledgeable than I and they tell me I will just return to the Land of Inspiration and remain there until I am called back again, if I am ever to be called back at all. I tell Zora these things, and she hugs me and promises she will never forget me. This reassures me, but every year I ask her to promise me again. I know the Land of Inspiration is a wonderful place, for I am always partially connected with it, but I wouldn't be able to live there without my Zora.

The robots inform me of the Sea of Interference and how the dark, shadowy creatures there will try to get Zora to forget me. They say that the Dove of Light, our master, stored a secret golden power within her, and the shadowy creatures will try to make her lose it. This is the only thing I fear, but I tell the robots that I will not let them near Zora. For some reason they laugh at me and shake their heads as they say, "Lucky, our friend, you cannot change fate. If Zora is to forget you, then the creatures of the Sea of Interference will have their way and make her forget. You won't even see them coming."

This of course saddens me, but I keep my hopes up and my spirits alive. I try to see the positive things in everything. Zora likes it when I sing to her. A song will come on the radio, and if she likes it, I will sing to her and dance. Through her mind I see her thinking of a story about a singing dog and his friends who start a band. It's a sort of silly story, but it's rather creative, so I encourage her to write it. She thinks about it sometimes, but she is only six years old now and waves the idea away.

Though Zora gets discouraged at times, she continues drawing and writing throughout school. There are many people throughout Zora's life that influence her. Some of them I love—like her second grade teacher Mrs. Gee, who got Zora signed up in writing competitions, and some of them I loathe. Zora and I are bored by one teacher in particular who speaks in a monotone voice—Mr. Leroy. Searching through his mind, I discover that he forgot his guardian and friend shortly after creating it. After discovering that saddening fact, I couldn't necessarily blame or scold Zora when she falls asleep in his class. Zora always seems to find good friends that I approve of because of their creative minds, and this makes me happy.

High school and boys are my enemies however, for they make Zora feel stressed and lightheaded, and I can't always get through to her. High school is robbing her of her creativity and turning her into an adult. The boy problem wouldn't be so bad, because I notice she works harder at her stories when she daydreams about a certain boy she had a crush on, but the creatures from the Sea of Interference sense her infatuation and take it as a weakness, and in turn, they sense the Golden Happiness at once, and they attack. It is just one shadowy creature, but it dwells inside her head with me and feasts upon any negative thoughts that it can find. I try to chase the shadowy figure out, but it is very strong. All I know is that I have to stay with my Zora.

Chapter 3

Zora

Lucky emerged from my head and was panting heavily. He lay down on the soft grass and closed his eyes. I realized the energy that it had cost him to show me that much of the story through his eyes. I stroked his head and as I did so, I thought about what I saw. I asked quietly, "I was the little girl? Was there really a monster inside my head from the Sea of Interference?"

Lucky opened one eye and murmured, "Yes, there was. It scared me, because I thought it was going to chase me away and make you forget me. I couldn't make it go away, but it wasn't because I was weak. It turned out the Sea of Interference was overpowering the Land of Inspiration at the time, and so all the creatures and their friends were being affected, but they came to you the most because of the Golden Happiness that the Dove of Light had stored within you. If you hadn't been so strong, I would've lost you. You were the only human who didn't lose her friend from the Land of Inspiration, and that's why this land and your old land didn't die. Can't you remember what happened? There was a big battle between you and the shadowy serpent."

I shook my head and said, "I'm sorry Lucky. I want to remember, for I know it makes you sad that I don't remember. I'm trying, but I just find it hard to imagine another land other than this one."

Lucky lifted his head slowly and looked at me. He gave me a weak smile and replied, "So long as you're trying to remember, little one. I'm sure you'll remember if I just send you the right memories. But Emily doesn't want you to remember. She's scared we won't be able to send you back if you remember and you want to return to your old home."

I kept Lucky's gaze and stroked his head and mused, "You called me little one. You're really concerned about me, aren't you? You want me to remember, yet at the same time you don't want me to because you're scared. Why?"

Lucky sighed, "Your missing heart piece worries me. I think the only way that it's possible to send you back to restore it is by making you remember. But if that doesn't work and you remember your past life then you'll live in eternal sadness. I saw the look on his face when you left. Everyone who was there realized the sacrifice you made for them, but he knew that you chose what you knew you had to because of him. He knew he was the reason you made the biggest sacrifice."

"Who was he?" I asked.

Lucky shook his head and slowly staggered to his feet. He looked at me for a long time and replied, "Maybe I should wait a little longer. I want you to tell me his name, for if you can do that, I'll know you finally have remembered."

I patted his head and said, "Okay, I'll trust you know what you're doing. Let's go down to the river and get you a drink. You look exhausted."

Lucky agreed and we walked across the wide meadow again and entered the forest that the deer had come out from. I followed the sound of rushing water and within minutes we had come to a river. A waterfall fed water to it and the sound of the rushing stream was pleasurable to listen to. The soft soil beneath my bare feet was cool and the lush greenness around me smelled heavenly. I rested my hand on a tree and felt its liveliness as Lucky lapped at the running water. I sighed and murmured, "This place feels so wonderful Lucky."

Lucky stopped drinking the water and pushed his nose in a nearby flower, a tiger lily. He inhaled the sweet scent and when he withdrew he turned to me and said, "I agree, but that is because I am with you. If I had to live here by myself, then it wouldn't be as great."

"But Lucky," I protested, "If you got me to remember what I'm supposed to be remembering, and you sent me back to where I supposedly came from, how would you survive here?"

Lucky looked at me, a startled expression on his face, as he exclaimed, "I would come with you of course! I would need to watch over you. Wouldn't that be okay?"

I shrugged, "You tell me. I accept your company now, but if you sent me back to who-knows-where, will I be the same?"

Lucky thought a bit, but then reassured me, "You would be the same, I'm sure of it. But you would have what your heart truly desires. Zora, do you know how old you are?"

I knelt down by the river and swished my finger in the running water. I pondered over Lucky's sudden question and murmured, "I'm not quite sure. I don't really know how much time passes here. I only know I've ruled this place all my life."

Lucky shook his head and said sternly, "You haven't been ruling this place all your life Zora. We've only made you believe that so that our worlds could be saved from the spreading of the Sea of Interference. No matter how many times I tell you though, you won't believe me until you remember what happened. It was the day of your graduation."

"Graduation? Graduation for what?" I was thoroughly confused.

Lucky had an expression of pity on his face as he answered quietly, "Graduation for high school, silly. You had to go through all those years of school just to have your heart broken and then get whisked away to this land. And you don't remember any of that?"

I shook my head and said, "School must've been a silly thing then. It's good I don't remember it. It seems like it was a waste of time the way you're putting it."

Lucky pattered away from the river bed and muttered, "It's not a waste of time in your world. What you learn in school helps you through the rest of your life. Zora, you would've been so successful, I'm sure of it, but we needed you here."

"So then keep me here. You still need me. What would happen if I went away? Wouldn't the creatures from the Sea of Interference just come back? Besides, I don't even know what this other world is."

I began to walk back out of the woods and Lucky followed me as he explained, "I think this world and your old one would be fine if you returned, your power has been growing since you've been here. Even if you were to leave, your power would still linger here and continue to grow as long as you live, and when you died in your old world, as everything does in that world, you would be able to return here and take your place as queen again. But there's no way I would send you back or could possibly send you back unless you remember."

I carefully picked my way through the trees and thick ferns and mumbled, "I still don't understand why the part of my heart that's 'turned black' is so important to you. I don't understand why it has to be restored if all it has done is caused me pain. I don't remember what pain it's caused, but according to Emily it was an unbearable pain."

Lucky was quiet for such a long time, I thought I had finally made my point, but as we emerged from the forest, he whispered sadly, "It has to be restored because it made you who you are. I feel like part of you is missing because one of your strongest emotions is gone." Lucky paused again before he continued even more quietly, "And I fear as if it was I who screwed things up for you. When the creature came to your mind, I couldn't fight him. He was so powerful that creature! And you were shy when talking to that boy at school, and so you talked to him on the computer at home instead, but your strong infatuations with him pushed me out of your mind, and then you were left to cope with the shadowy monster yourself. The monster made your mind cloudier than ever, and sometimes you said the wrong things, and I was not there for you. I was a weak and lousy friend ..."

I stopped in my tracks quickly and spun around. Then I grabbed him by the scruff of his neck and said sharply, "Lucky! You are not a lousy friend! You keep me company and make me happy. Perhaps you couldn't fight the terrible monsters that came to me, but you tried, and that's all that matters ... you did your best to protect me. I don't even remember my past life, so stop blaming yourself for something that doesn't matter."

Lucky pulled away from me and growled, "But it does matter, Zora! You are not yourself, and I miss my old Zora! I love and respect you because you are a kind queen, but I wish your heart wasn't missing. I loved the foolish you, Zora! Don't you remember how madly in love you were with that boy? You wanted just one date with him, but because of me being weak you never got that chance. You did some silly things because of him. You were more determined then ever to be successful in life just so that he would once look at you with admiring eyes. But I took you away before you had that chance, and I regret it to this day! I wish I had found someone else to do the task appointed for you! But the Dove of Light … the Dove of Light—He is master and I am only …"

He trailed off and I was astonished to see that tears were streaming down his cheeks. I knelt down and opened my arms to hug him. He slowly walked towards me and I embraced him in a warm hug. As I stroked his fur, I murmured, "Lucky, this is twice today that you've cried. I'm sorry that the fact that I don't remember bothers you so much. I'll try hard to remember, but I understand it might make me sad. Let's go to the castle for a nap. You can tell me more of your story once you've rested up. I feel you are worn out."

Lucky buried his head against my chest and sniffed, "Thank you Zora. I'm sorry I'm being so troublesome today, but I really want you to find your lost heart piece. You're just not the same without it."

I slowly withdrew from him and then stood up. I looked down at him and smiled. He returned the smile weakly and then we headed towards the castle. When we were at the bridge again, a hedgehog was sitting on the middle of the bridge, stroking its fur with one paw and holding a mirror in its other paw. Lucky looked at the hedgehog quizzically and then at me. I shrugged and then called out, "Oh Miss Hedgehog! Is there something you require of me, or are you just passing by?"

The hedgehog stopped running her paw through her fur and set the mirror down. Then she looked up at me and a smile stretched across her face and she exclaimed, "Oh! Queen Zora, there you are! Emily ran into me a few minutes ago with a look of urgency on her face. I asked her what the fuss was about and she just mumbled something about a diary and if the right someone reads it the door to the other world can be opened … whatever that means. When she noticed I was sitting there, a look of horror crossed her face and she told me not to tell anyone what she just said. I thought she was up to no good, so I came here to tell you."

Before I could say anything, Lucky jumped towards the hedgehog and asked excitedly, "Is that all she said? By other world, did she mean Zora's old world? What diary needs to be read?"

The hedgehog recoiled away from Lucky and replied scornfully, "I'm not sure what diary needs to be read and I'm not sure which other world Emily was talking about. It all sounded like nonsense to me, but I thought if anyone could make any sense of it, it would be Queen Zora.

You are very rude you know? Butting into a conversation like you did—I wasn't even talking to you!"

Lucky backed up and when he was standing by my side again, he said gruffly, "Sorry Mrs. Hedgehog, I didn't mean to. Please accept my apology."

The hedgehog nodded towards Lucky, but was still glaring at him. When she returned her gaze to me, her look softened and she stated, "I hope you find out if Emily's up to no good. It really made me feel suspicious the way she ran off like she did. Good day to you Queen Zora."

The hedgehog picked up her mirror with her mouth and began to waddle away across the meadow. I called after her, "Thank you for the information Mrs. Hedgehog! Good day!"

The hedgehog turned her head and nodded in my direction and then continued on her way. When I returned my gaze to Lucky, he muttered, "I knew Emily knew more than what she let on. Zora, don't you see? Emily knows how to send you back, but she doesn't want to let you go. She's being selfish. That's why she's been keeping such close guard on you."

I shook my head and said, "Back to where though, Lucky?"

Lucky opened his mouth to answer, but then closed it again as a look of comprehension suddenly crossed his face. He blurted out, "Remembering *must* be part of the key of sending you back! That's why Emily was so upset when I was telling you those stories. She's afraid if you remember I will be able to send you back, and she doesn't want you to leave, but why? What would it matter?"

I shrugged and said, "I still haven't the slightest idea what you're talking about, but I assume Emily doesn't want me to go away, because if the stories you're telling me are true, maybe she fears the creatures from the Sea of Interference will come back."

Lucky looked at me for a while and yawned, "Maybe you're right, but I think Emily's up to something. I'll think about it more after my nap. Will you be joining me?"

I nodded and led Lucky through the castle door. Instead of going up the stairs like the time before, I went through a door on the right. Lucky pattered softly behind me and we entered a dark soothing room. There was one window where sunlight poured in. The walls to this room were gray and the white fluffy bed had purple drapes around it.

The luxurious black carpeting felt comforting on my feet. The bed was large enough for me stretch out on and for Lucky to curl up at my feet and have plenty of room to sleep contentedly at the same time. The room was empty, save the bed.

Lucky looked around at the room and then jumped up on the bed as he said, "This room is an example of how you've changed, Zora. You would have never put up with such a boring room. There's nothing in here."

As Lucky walked around in circles before curling up on the bed, I replied, "I don't really see why I need anything in here though. I'm not in here very often. All the exciting stuff is outside. Why crowd a room with silly knickknacks when all it will do is collect dust?"

Lucky gave me a strange look and questioned, "Dust? Zora, there is no dust in this world that gathers on knickknacks—this is a clean world. Could it be you're starting to remember?" I was about to protest that I hadn't remembered anything, but Lucky cut me off and mumbled, "Never you mind little one. Get some sleep and when we awaken we shall eat and then I shall continue our story."

I climbed into the bed and pulled the soft blankets over me, but for some reason, no matter how hard I tried, I couldn't fall asleep. I sat staring at the purple drapes and how the sun shined on them and the bed and warmed me. Normally this helped me to fall asleep, but I was restless all of a sudden. Why did Lucky want me to retrieve my lost heart all of a sudden? Did its absence pain him terribly? As I listened to his gentle snoring, I heard a meow from outside and smiled. I looked towards the open window and saw a small, fluffy creature sitting on the windowsill.

The creature had large, round, blue eyes and had a head resembling that of a panda. Her fur was soft and curly like wool and she had large purple paws. Other than her paws and the black markings on her face, she was a pure white color.

"Hey Pooky," I greeted, "I suppose you sensed that I couldn't sleep when I wanted to sleep and came to help, huh?"

Pooky cocked her head and then leapt down from the windowsill ever so lightly. She then plodded over to the bed and jumped up next to me. As soon as she had landed on the bed, a sweet scent of lavender drifted from her, and I began to grow drowsy. Pooky curled up on my stomach and began to purr contentedly. I stroked her soft wool and within minutes, I had drifted off to sleep.

Chapter 4

Zora

Hours later, I woke with a start to the sounds of Lucky growling. I rubbed my eyes and sat up, realizing that Pooky was no longer on my stomach, but on the windowsill and hissing. Lucky was below the windowsill and his fur was standing on end. I quickly got out of bed and mumbled sleepily, "Lucky, leave Pooky alone. She's only here because I had trouble getting to sleep."

I walked over to where Lucky was standing and he turned to me with a start and stammered, "Sorry Zora. It's just that … well; you know how much I hate things that purr. Pooky sounds too much like a cat. It woke me up. Sorry if I woke you, I didn't mean to growl."

I shook my head but a smile spread across my face as I said, "Ah Lucky, when will I get you to behave? No matter, I can't yell at you for being a dog."

Lucky shot a glaring look towards Pooky, causing Pooky to jump out of the window. When Lucky returned his gaze to me, he was somber and he said, "But Zora, I'm more than just a silly dog. I've got a little human in me too, like all creatures of the Land of Inspiration. You know that I'm able to control my anger towards purring things most of the time; it's just that Pooky startled me by just suddenly appearing."

I rubbed Lucky's head and replied with a smile, "Well I'm sorry to break it to you Lucky, but Pooky had been here for quite some time I believe before you woke up."

Lucky shrugged and answered, "Well I guess I just realized her purring when sleep was beginning to wear off, but Pooky wasn't there when I went to sleep, so I have an excuse for jumping at her so."

I began to walk out of the room and Lucky followed as I said, "Okay, so you have an excuse. What should we do now though? Perhaps climb to the peaks of some mountains?"

We walked out of the castle and Lucky responded, "If climbing mountains is what you want to do, I'm all for it."

Before, if Lucky would have said this to me, I would've instantly started off for the mountains, but now his response made me hesitate. Everything he did was to please me, and I just realized it now. The fact that he wanted me to remember something that, to me, seemed clearly impossible got me worrying. It was the same reason why I couldn't fall asleep before. I stopped and turned to face Lucky with a smile as I said, "You know what? Why don't you pick what we do now?"

Lucky looked taken aback, for he stammered, "Well, I ... um ... you've never asked me what we should do before. Why now?"

"Well Lucky," I replied, "You are my best friend. I think it would be fair to say that it's your turn to make a decision for once. I mean, I only have eternity to spend in this place, so why not switch it up a bit?"

Lucky pondered this for a while before he answered, "You're my best friend too, Zora, and that's why I'm helping you get your missing heart piece back. You don't realize it's gone, but I do. It's causing me more grief and pain then when the shadowy creatures from the Sea of Interference were here."

I stared at Lucky for a while and then asked quietly, "How much pain did the shadowy creatures cause?"

Lucky again looked deep in thought as if choosing his words wisely. Finally he responded, "A lot. That's why I had to drag you here from your old world. Believe me; all the creatures here knew the sacrifice that you would have to make. That's why they had to wipe your memory away—so you wouldn't be in pain with your memories and regrets, but they didn't know it would cause you to lose part of your heart as well."

I watched Lucky for a while, waiting for him to go on and tell me what he wanted to do. When he didn't say anything more, I began walking across the meadow again. Actually it was more like wandering—I didn't have a specific place I had to be at any time. My life was carefree. Lucky broke the silence by exclaiming, "Oh! I've got an idea on what we can do! Conrad Silverscales could show you what happened. He can show you how he first discovered a cloud from the Sea of Interference in this land. And maybe if you're lucky, he will show you his battle he had with one of the shadowy creatures. Conrad Silverscales was the last creature here to give up. He gave me the final order to get you."

I kept slowly walking away as I said, "I still don't know why you keep talking about this 'getting me' nonsense, but if it would please you to have me listen to him, then I will."

Lucky stated sadly, "I am hoping this will make you realize you were not always here. You were somewhere else; you were in the world that we creatures here protect from despair."

The grief of his voice made me worry once more and so I replied gently, "Lucky, I am trying to remember what you want me to, but it's just so hard. All I have is your memories of what I was like before, but since I don't remember that, how can I ever recall? I hope for your happiness, I will remember, but I can't make any promises."

Lucky sniffled and said, "I know, Zora. I'm just so frustrated, but Conrad may be able to help." Then he looked up towards the sky and barked three quick notes and then cried out, "Conrad Silverscales! I require your presence!"

I looked up at the sky and across the horizon, but saw only an empty sky with a few passing birds. No dragon. I waited a few more minutes before saying, "Lucky, I don't think he's coming. Maybe he didn't hear y—"

"Shush!" Lucky interrupted, "Listen Zora. He is coming."

I heard a joyful roar and suddenly I saw a flashing speck of silver off towards the northern mountains. Conrad must've been traveling at a hasty speed, because within seconds, his vast shadow was over Lucky and me. As he flapped his wings and skimmed low, just above my head, a large wind gust buffeted me, ruffling my hair and my dress. Conrad turned sharply and then landed at my side and bowed his head in greeting. In turn, I said, "Good day to you Conrad. How have you been since we last met?"

Conrad flashed me a toothy grin and replied, "I am well. The sun is keeping my energy up. Did you want to fly with me again?"

I shook my head and Lucky stepped in then and explained, "Queen Zora would like you to show her the battle between you and the shadowy creatures."

Conrad looked at me, a curious expression on his face as he asked, "Is that so?"

I nodded and added, "I hear you fought very bravely. Will you show me your strength through your memories?"

Conrad held his head up proudly as he said with confidence, "Of course, if that is what you wish. You will have to lie down though and close your eyes. Relax your mind and I will show you my epic battle."

I did as told and I felt his spirit begin to pour through my head. A million memories flashed through my mind and when they slowed down, I was looking through the eyes of the silver-scaled dragon, Conrad.

Chapter 5

Conrad Silverscales

I had been enjoying my day in the Land of Inspiration. Of course, I knew the Sea of Interference was growing stronger with each passing moment, but I had no idea it would soon break into my homeland.

It started with a faint storm cloud off into the distance. I, being of the curious sort, flew off at once to see what it was. When I flew to the cloud, however, I realized it was on the ground. I landed and sniffed the cloud, and fear rose up inside me when I smelled salt and mold. I backed away from the cloud, and raised my head to the sky, letting out a warning roar.

Emily the unicorn was the first one to answer my call. She trotted up to me and asked, "What is it, Conrad Silverscales? Why such a fearful sound? What worries you?" Before I could reply, Emily caught the scent of the cloud and backed away quickly. She cried out, "The Sea of Interference! It is here!"

I nodded and asked, "What do we do, Emily? I fear the shadowy creatures will emerge from this cloud of darkness any second. We will have to fight them in order to prevent their evilness from seeping into the other world."

Other creatures began to emerge from forests and meadows. They all looked at the dark cloud with the same fear that Emily and I felt. Emily looked at the crowd around us and said with a slight tremor in her voice, "We cannot let this land fall to their darkness, or both this world and the humans' world will be destroyed."

The creatures stared at her with wide eyes, and a large buffalo protested with a gruff voice, "We will fight to save our lands, but what if the shadowy creatures won't go away?"

Before Emily or I could respond, a crocodile with six legs retorted, "Mr. Buffalo sir, the shadowy creatures are not even here yet. I say we should not worry; perhaps this cloud will go away."

A mouse with spikes on its back piped in, "I agree with Miss Crocodile. Although, our master would most likely want us to destroy this cloud of evil darkness as soon as possible."

I stated, "Aye, our master would most likely want that, but how do we destroy it? Furthermore, how did it even get here?"

There was a brief silence, and then chaos erupted as all the creatures surrounding the cloud began to shout out answers.

"Perhaps Conrad Silverscales should breathe fire on it!"

"No, that won't work. We must bury it in a field of daisies!"

"Nay, I say throw it in a lake!"

"That will just foul the waters. Don't you see that we have to send it back from where it came from?"

The shouting went on for nearly five minutes before Emily finally cried out, "*Enough!*" The creatures instantly grew silent, and Emily huffed, "Finally. Okay, we all know this cloud is from the Sea of Interference—we can all smell the uncleanness, and we have to somehow make it disappear, but—"

"I do say!" An owl suddenly exclaimed, cutting Emily off, "Did that cloud just get bigger?"

We all looked at the cloud and realized it had indeed grown since we first came upon it. The creatures were all stunned, paralyzed by fear. Emily opened and closed her mouth several times before she breathed, "Oh my. This is indeed very bad. We must call the Dove of Light, our master, at once. He will know what to do."

The other creatures and I all murmured our agreement, and Emily began walking toward a lone building—a castle. We followed quickly and quietly behind her, and when we reached the castle, we formed a circle around it and began to sing:

"Oh Creator of Happiness and Light,
we call for you to calm and soothe the fright,
the fright we feel this very day,
the fright we wish would go away."

A great light came from directly above the castle, and a snow-white dove descended from the clouds. He perched on the top of the castle as all the creatures began to gather on one side of the castle so He could see us all at once. He looked upon us with gentle eyes and asked in a deep, friendly voice, "What troubles you, protectors of happiness? What goes awry in my land of peace?"

Emily stepped forward and answered, "Conrad Silverscales found a cloud of darkness today in this Land of Inspiration. While we were discussing a way to get rid of it, it has grown almost double its size. It smells rancid and penetrates fear into our hearts."

The Dove of Light looked startled, but then He sighed heavily and said, "I assumed it would only be a matter of time. The shadowy creatures want to break into this land, for they know that if they have control of this land, then the humans will be next. They enjoy torturing humans."

I raised my head to Him and asked, "Is there no way we can send it back? Will the Sea of Interference destroy us all?"

The Dove of Light looked alarmed at my doubtfulness, and He exclaimed, "Now then! What is this mixture of doubt and fear that runs through your veins? Do you think I would just let this land fall and then let the human race live in shadows? Nay, you are great guardians, and I have prepared for the worst. Over the past twelve or so years, I have sensed the evil Serpent of Darkness was growing in power and strength, and so I have bestowed a golden power into a human girl. The loyal guardian that I gave to her when she was born is a golden retriever named Lucky. You must summon him and tell him to bring the girl home. Only he can bring her here."

Emily questioned, "Who is this girl you speak of? How will her power help us? I do not quite understand."

The Dove of Light replied, "She is just an ordinary human, but she has the Golden Gift that I bestowed upon her. Her creativity is boundless, and her optimism is unending. When the shadowy creatures see her, they will at once be afraid and will be sent whimpering back to their shadowy sea from whence they came. But alas! Her power can only be unleashed in this land. If the shadowy creatures find that hidden power while she is still in her world, they will try to destroy her. You must persuade Lucky to bring her here, or all will perish."

"How will we summon him?"

"Inside the castle, there is a green door. When you open it, you will see a vast blue sky, and you must call out, 'Lucky, Keeper of the Daughter of Light, come home for a visit to the Land of Inspiration!' I am counting on you to keep the shadow of doubt from spreading. I must now prepare myself to attack the Serpent of Darkness if you should fail to retrieve the girl."

Emily bowed, and the rest of us followed suit as Emily said, "We shall not disappoint you, oh great one."

The Dove of Light smiled and then spread His wings. He flew up from where He came from, and when the light died down, He was gone. We stood in silence for a while before Emily said, "Well, let us call upon this Lucky then, shall we?"

Two white, egg-shaped creatures with robotic voices emerged from the crowd just then. They floated slightly above the ground and had a learned look in their black eyes. They reminded me of something like ghosts, but they were not transparent. They said in unison, "We remember who Lucky is. He is with Zora, who must be the keeper of this great power that the Dove of Light speaks of. Zora had a brother named Bradley who we stayed with until he forgot us. Then we returned here, as all creatures eventually do. Let us call for Lucky. He will trust us and come."

Emily nodded toward the two creatures, and they entered the castle. We watched them find the green door and then held our breath when they opened it. They chanted, "Lucky, Keeper of the Daughter of Light, come home for a visit to the Land of Inspiration!"

At first there was no answer, and the creatures around me began to disperse. But then there was a loud piercing sound and a whooshing noise as a golden retriever shot out of the door. He landed on the ghosts, and they fell down with a cry of "Oomph!" When the dog, Lucky, got up, he looked at the ghosts apologetically and then glanced out the castle. When he saw us all, his face filled with confusion, and he asked, "What's going on here? Why have I been summoned?"

Emily approached him cautiously and said slowly, "Lucky, you may or may not know it, but you are the guardian of a very special girl."

Lucky looked at Emily quizzically and replied, "I know that. Zora has lots of talents. I need to go back to her though, or she'll worry."

Emily shook her head in frustration and then explained more hastily, "No, Lucky. We need your human here. A dark shadow has come to this land from the Sea of Interference, and the Dove of Light told us that your girl can make the shadowy creatures go away. She needs to get here as quickly as possible, for she has had the Golden Gift bestowed upon her, but it can only be unleashed in this land. The Dove of Light told us all this, and He also said that if the shadowy creatures spot the power in her and she is not here in this land, they will try to destroy her."

Lucky hesitated, and I saw him back away from us, as if he planned to run away. Emily gave him a hard stare, and he whimpered, "You mean to take Zora away from her home? Think about all the people who will be affected! How can you ask me to do something like that? Just tell the Dove of Light to move the power to someone else."

Emily retorted harshly, "He cannot so easily move the power! If so, I'm sure he would so we wouldn't have to put up with your whining. If she is not brought here immediately, the whole Land of Inspiration will be doomed, and in turn, so will her world. We are not taking her away from *you*, so why is this simple wish so hard for you to grant?"

I interceded here, noticing how Emily's bitter tone was frustrating Lucky, and said, "Perhaps, Emily, we should try fighting this cloud ourselves. The Dove of Light never said that we couldn't. That way, we won't have to interfere with this human's life."

Emily pondered this for a while, and then a voice called out, "Aye! We are stronger than these shadows, Emily! We don't need to disturb a human's life just because we are frightened!"

Emily and I glanced to where the voice had come from. We saw a white dinosaur-like creature with black stripes like that of a zebra. He stood upright on his muscular hind legs. His claws on his feet and forearms appeared sharp. He had ears like a dog, and his lower jaw jutted out over his upper lip, so that his razor-sharp teeth stuck out over his upper lip. Drool dripped from the corner of his mouth, which would have given him a dim-witted appearance had it not been for his golden eyes that glimmered sharply with a strong cunningness. He looked at Emily with a spark of viciousness in his eyes and said boldly, "We are strong! Together, we can push these shadowy creatures back from where they came!"

The creatures around him cheered. His sudden optimism seemed to latch on to the others quickly. When the creatures were quiet again, Emily stated, "All right, we will try to fight them, but if they take our sun, then we will become immobile. So we will have to make sure to call Lucky and his girl before that happens."

The creatures around her nodded their agreement. She turned to Lucky and said, "You may return to your girl now, but the next time we call for you, you must bring her here—no questions asked. Agreed?"

Lucky paused for a long while, but finally, seeing there was no other choice, he sighed, "Fine. I agree to bring her here the next time you ask, even though I fear what will happen to her and the people who know her."

Emily smiled warmly at him and said, "Good, you may go."

Lucky nodded to her and then turned back toward the open green door and jumped through it. He vanished through a blinding flash of light and another loud piercing sound. When the light died down, and the ghosts closed the door, Emily said, "Well then … let us see what we can do about this cloud of darkness, shall we?"

The creatures and I murmured our agreement, and Emily continued, "Right. Make sure *all* the creatures of this land have been notified of the cloud's presence, so that none is taken off guard by the sudden appearance of the monsters. Most of us were present at the meeting of the Dove of Light, but I am aware that this land is large so not all the creatures may have heard Conrad's roar. Off with you now!"

The creatures all quickly scrambled away to spread the message and to prepare for battle. I stayed with Emily, however, and asked, "Are you ready for this battle, Emily?"

Emily looked at me, and I could feel her fear—as well as see it in her eyes—but she said with an unwavering and determined voice, "Let us stop this evilness once and for all! I am ready."

I smiled and spread my wings, preparing to take flight. Emily looked at me with a questioning stare, and I said, "I will make sure the shadowy creatures don't take us off guard. I will watch that cloud and attack the first thing that comes out of it. I will make sure *I* have the upper hand."

As I launched myself into the sky, Emily yelled from below, "Be careful, Conrad Silverscales! Call for us when the first shadowy creature comes!"

I began flooding my conscience with the strongest positive thoughts I could, knowing that the shadowy creatures would be weakened against the glow that optimism would create. I angled down towards where the dark cloud was and landed next to it. The stench of the cloud was almost unbearable, but I stood by, nonetheless, and watched it.

I sat there for many hours, and fear grabbed hold of me when I could see the cloud growing, but Emily suddenly appeared at my side and soothed, "Conrad Silverscales, all will be well if you don't let this thing frighten you. We have the advantage of the bright sun on our side, and all of the creatures have been notified. Millions will be fighting, and we will continue to fight until the shadows blot out the sun, or until we have won."

I nodded, comforted by her words, and took a deep breath, but then I heard the moan. It was a deep, grumbling, frightful moan. It came from the cloud, and I tensed up and growled at it. The moan sounded again, more loudly than before, and Emily reared up and neighed loudly, signaling to the other creatures that the shadows were nearly upon us. I didn't know if all heard her, so I joined my fervent roar with her musical neigh, and the sound echoed across the hills and valleys of the Land of Inspiration.

I didn't have time to find out what creatures answered the battle cry first, because at that instant, a great shadowy creature emerged from the cloud. It was made up from the same material the cloud was—it was dark with gleaming red eyes and it seemed to have no definite form. It smelled of rotting wood and mold, and when it looked at me, its shape began to imitate my own. I was startled when the black cloud with gleaming red eyes suddenly looked like a dragon. It looked at me and let out an ear-piercing cry, its dark billowy mouth like a deep abyss, and its teeth were just as dark and cloudy.

Next to me, Emily's horn began to glow brightly, and sparks were beginning to form at its tip, but before she could attack, I lunged at the shadow-like dragon and my positive glow clashed with its negative cloud with brute force. It became a tangled mess of claws and teeth—my glowing ones against its shadowy ones. The sun shone brightly in the sky and I knew the Dove of Light was giving me the sudden surge of energy I felt. The brightness also weakened the shadow dragon, and within minutes, I was able to push it back through the cloud from whence it came. But the battle was not over then; more shadowy creatures had come from the cloud while I had been fighting the dragon, and my friends below were fighting them. The shadowy creatures that fought took the shape of the good creatures that were against them. I was awed by this and puzzled at the same time. Then I shook myself of the confusing emotions I was sure the shadowy creatures were casting on me, and started towards another shadowy creature.

I clashed into this one with the same amount of power as the first, and it took the shape of a dragon, as the first did. I was victorious again, but only to be faced with another shadow …

Chapter 6

Zora

I opened my eyes when I felt Conrad's conscience pulling away from mine. When I sat up, he was in a heap at my side, and breathing heavy as Lucky had been when he emerged from my head earlier.

I stood up quickly and walked towards his massive head, which was lying on the lush grass. I placed my hand on his brow and asked in a concerned voice, "Why does going into my conscience make you creatures so tired when nothing else seems to affect your energy?"

Conrad opened his eyes and smiled weakly as he explained, "It is dark in one's conscience; the sun does not shine there; that is why I tire. It is not dark when your eyes are open, but if they were not closed when I entered, you would not be able to see my memories. Do not feel bad Zora, it happens to all creatures no matter whose conscience they enter. Besides, I was pleased to show you that part of the battle."

I was relieved to hear him talking, for that meant he was well and would recover quickly, but I couldn't stop myself from asking, "But Conrad, what happened afterwards? I only saw the beginning of the battle."

Conrad picked up his head from the grass and replied, "Well, the battle with the shadowy creatures went on for many days. About three years in the human world, and suddenly the Serpent of Darkness emerged from the cloud. He had poisonous purple rays surrounding his black shadowy body. His red eyes gleamed with an evilness that petrified nearly all of us, but I looked away from him, for Emily had called out my name. She had cried, 'Conrad Silverscales! Do not look into the serpent's eyes! You must call Lucky! It is time.'" Conrad paused a long while and he shuddered before he continued, "When I looked at Emily after she had said this, I noticed she had become suddenly still, and the power that the serpent had begun to drain from me was returning. Emily was lending me what little strength she had so that I could call Lucky and his girl ... which is you, Zora."

I stared at Conrad and murmured, "So it is true. I am from a different world—I saw Lucky come from it in your memories. But why haven't I any memories of my own of the other world?" I hesitated, and then continued in a low voice, "I don't remember my home ... I don't remember where I belong."

Conrad looked taken aback, and he exclaimed, "But Zora! You belong here now—you're not supposed to remember your old home. We erased it from your mind so you would be happy here. Surely if you try to remember your old home, you will grow homesick, and we creatures here are not sure how to send you back."

I thought about what Conrad said, and then looked around for Lucky, realizing I had not seen him since before Conrad told his tale. His absence suddenly worried me, as if he being away was like a part of me being absent. Conrad caught my anxious expression and wondered aloud, "Well now! Where has your friend and guardian, Lucky, gone?"

I shrugged and said, "He's been acting rather peculiar lately—he wants me to remember what other creatures here want to stay forgotten. He says I'm missing part of my heart and it pains him. Something to do with a boy in my old world ... my home I guess."

Conrad got to his feet and craned his neck high up towards the sky and sun. He hummed contentedly and stated, "Ah, the sun is nice and my energy is up again. But what do you say about a missing heart piece? I know nothing of humans' hearts, but from what I heard of other creatures who have visited people in your home, hearts are a troublesome thing. My human forgot me quite quickly, so I never got to know about the complications of such things."

I rubbed my hand lightly on Conrad's scales and then said, "You speak of creatures here going to my old world, and I saw from your memories that the robot-ghost creatures were friends with … with my brother? I knew not that I had a brother, but it must be true. But what did the ghosts mean when they say they returned here when Bradley forgot them?"

Conrad scratched his neck with his front claw and replied, "Hmm … this is a complicated thing to explain. You see, all the creatures here have been in your old world, responsible for protecting a child with abundant imagination and good thoughts … an innocent child if you will. The child determines what we look like and how long we are able to stay with them. When the child grows older and bores of us 'imaginary friends,' or so what we're called since we only make ourselves known to our child, we come to this land and wait for them to finish out their lives. We protect them from where we are by remembering their minds, and sending them ideas on how to make their lives successful—more of like a conscience or a guardian angel, if you will. Sometimes they listen to us, and sometimes they don't. Anyway, when they die in that world, they come here and reunite with whichever friend they had formed long ago and then together, they go up into the sun, and what happens after that I can only guess. Rumor has it that there is a wonderful home up there for humans and guardians alike—kind of like this place—but those who go have never come back, so I do not know. The robot-ghosts are still here, waiting patiently for Bradley to finish his life. All creatures here are just waiting."

The information Conrad was giving me was interesting, but I was a bit confused by it all, and then it occurred to me why. "Conrad," I asked, "Why aren't I up there in the sun then with other people? Why are Lucky and I stuck in this … this 'waiting room?'"

Conrad suddenly spread out his wings and his muscles tensed up as if he was about to fly away, but I held him steadfast with my unwavering and questioning gaze, and he finally answered regretfully, "Zora, you are the Dove of Light's chosen one. This is your home now; you are in charge of watching over his guardian angels … in charge of watching over us. You are not in the sun because you are not dead … you are forever immortal and will stay here until the human race has ended and your old world has been destroyed. You will never age here. You are stuck at eighteen years old for eternity. Good day to you, Queen Zora."

Before I could protest, Conrad had taken off, and I was left alone. I watched him as he disappeared behind the great mountains, and for the first time, I felt lonely. I looked around and saw a rabbit like creature with a fox's tail. It had a black ninja mask tied around its head with holes cut out where its eyes were peering out of. It walked on two legs, yet bounded over to me and landed on four. Its whiskers tickled my feet as the creature sniffed me. I wanted to laugh, but since Lucky was not present, it did not seem right. The creature spoke in a quick but concerned voice, "Queen Zora? Are you okay? You do not look well."

I patted the creature's head and responded, "I am fine, Mushookie, but thanks for your concern." I paused and saw that my answer did not convince Mushookie, and so I asked, "Have you seen Lucky? It worries me that he is gone."

Mushookie looked thoughtful and then he replied, "I believe I saw him talking with Emily in the valley between two mountains where a river rushes by. I could take you there if you would like."

I was about to say yes, but then I remembered whenever Lucky talked to Emily it was usually an argument about me. I didn't want to listen to them babble, and I was really curious about the ghost creatures, so I asked, "Actually Mushookie, do you think you could get two creatures for me? I don't know their names, but they kind of look like ghosts and speak in robotic voices. And … and they were friends with a human named Bradley."

Mushookie looked at me with a shocked expression and spluttered, "You're not supposed to remember your brother!"

I held up a hand to silence him and said calmly, "Don't worry Mushookie, I don't remember him. I've only heard his name. But can you get his friends for me? I would like to speak with them."

Mushookie sighed and said, "Very well, I shall get them. You are Queen, after all."

Mushookie hopped back up on two feet and sprang away. While I waited, I looked up at the bright sun and suddenly understood why it never sank. It was a different world that somehow gave energy to the creatures of the Land of Inspiration. But why did I never see the great Dove of Light? I thought about this for a while and then figured it must be because He lived in the sun and only came down once in a while. But then why didn't He tell the guardians what was in the Sun of

Happiness? I shrugged it off and decided it didn't really matter. I would most likely never see it.

When Mushookie returned, he had with him, as I had asked, the two ghost-like creatures I saw from Conrad's memories. Mushookie sat on a rock nearby while the ghosts asked simultaneously, "Yes, Queen Zora? We hear you required our company … can we help you with anything?"

I looked at them and noted, "You two talk at the same time always, as if you were one."

The ghosts nodded and then replied together, "It is because we belong to the same human. Some humans have more than one imaginary friend on Earth, but when they are forgotten and come here, they join together as one."

"More than one imaginary friend?" I questioned, "Did I ever have more than one? If I did, where is it now?"

The ghosts replied calmly, "Yes, you did sometimes think of other creatures to keep Lucky company when you were on Earth, but they changed so much and they didn't stick around. You were always thinking up of new things, but Lucky was always there. Anyway, humans technically only have one conscience that they listen to."

I hesitated before asking, "And Bradley's your human then? He was my brother … and he forgot you?"

Now it was the ghosts' turn to pause, but they answered, "Yes, Bradley is our human. Do you remember him, Zora?" I shook my head and they continued, "Well, I suppose that's for the better. He was a very creative boy, but all little children forget their friends sooner or later. You haven't forgotten Lucky because you are the chosen one."

I murmured solemnly, "Why was it me who was chosen? I don't understand."

They shrugged and then answered, "Nobody really knows why the Dove of Light does what he does. Perhaps you are the keeper of the Golden Happiness only by random selection, or because the Dove of Light saw something in you that others did not have. All we really know for certain is that while you watch over this land, more creatures that are being forgotten are coming to this land, and the humans who have forgotten and died are reuniting with their old guardians and going to the Sun of Happiness."

"So it is true," I stated flatly, "I am not dead."

The ghosts looked at each other uncertainly, but they said slowly, "We cannot lie to you Queen Zora, that would be cruel. You are not dead, it is true, but do not think of it as punishment. Why do these trifles bother you? They never used to."

I shrugged. I'm not sure how to answer, for I did not know the answer myself. I broke the long silence by saying, "That is all I wanted to know … I suppose. You may go now."

The ghosts bowed to me and said, "Good day to you, Zora." And then they left. Mushookie, however, stayed and was eyeing me again with a curious expression.

He spoke before I could ask if he wanted anything. He said, "Queen Zora, for as long as you've been here, I don't believe you've ever seen a creature reunite with its human. Would you like to see?"

I was skeptical, "How?"

Mushookie stood up on his hind legs and replied, "Come with me, you will see. Old Miss Crocodile's human is about to pass away. Hurry now or you'll miss it."

With a bound and a leap, Mushookie was off, and I rushed after him. We traveled across many meadows and then we came upon a dark, misty forest. It was different from the other forest that Lucky and I had gone to, but it still smelled as pleasant. The warm sun beat down on the soggy ground and when we reached a swamp filled with lilies; I saw an old green crocodile with six legs. I stared at her for a while in disbelief—this was the exact same crocodile in Conrad's memories. I suddenly knew how I could figure out how many years I was supposed to be, had I not been stuck at eighteen.

"Miss Crocodile," I began, "How long has it been since the Great Battle with the shadowy creatures?"

The crocodile, which had been sleeping, lazily opened her eyes and answered in a weak, but still friendly voice, "Ah, Queen Zora. I knew your memory wouldn't be erased for eternity. Years are not the same in your world as they are here, for the sky never changes—the sun never moves. But do not worry; you have not been here long. I was already old in the Great Battle. My human was fighting cancer—a terrible tragedy. By the end of his human day, he will be with me and we will go up to the Sun of Happiness and see what awaits us."

I was somewhat surprised. This crocodile spoke as though she knew what I was worrying about. The crocodile continued, "I do not know why you would want to go back to your old world—it is not as carefree as this one, but to reassure you I will say this: I have been keeping track of how long the shadowy creatures have been away. They will always be scared of your power, no matter what. You are still young Zora, but you have the wisdom of the old."

The crocodile began to close her eyes, and she started to glow brightly. She had begun to answer my worries, but she had not finished what I wanted to know most at that moment. I cried out, "Wait! How old am I then? How old would I be in … in my old world?"

Her eyes shot open and she said quickly as the glow began to intensify, "You are twenty, Zora. You have been here for only two years in your old world's time. Oh, but what is time when you are immortal? Never mind me though, goodbye Queen Zora, you are a fine ruler, but it is my time at last."

"But," I protested, "I feel as though I've been here all my life!"

The crocodile closed her eyes and the light was so bright, I could not see her, but I heard her faint voice reply, "You have not, but you must remember on your own to get back to your old world, if you really desire that place. Now, this is farewell, Queen Zora."

Suddenly, there was a figure beside the glowing light that engulfed the crocodile, a human figure, but it was glowing too, so I could not see what the person was like. The two glowing figures began to rise up into the sky and they merged into one. The brightness was so beautiful! But it was over in seconds; the light went up to the sun and then seemed to just disappear.

I looked at Mushookie and abruptly demanded, "How come this is the first time I have seen this? I've been here for two years!"

Mushookie shrugged and answered calmly, "Well, this land *is* vast, and many of the creatures are in deep parts of the forest, so they can reunite with their humans in peace. Besides, you don't know how many of the Land of Inspiration days are equal to one of your old world's years. Days are hard to count here, for it never gets dark, and the sun never moves. Perhaps you have not been here as long as you think you have."

I began walking out of the forest and Mushookie followed me. I asked him as I walked, "Okay, so how long have you been here? How long ago did your human forget you? And why is it that for as long as

I've been here, suddenly just now some creatures are wanting me to remember my past life?"

Mushookie replied, "I've been here for only a short while. You were here before I was forgotten. Only the creatures who are tied to you in some way want you to remember ... they must feel the brokenness inside. I am young and I am not your closest friend as Lucky is, so that is why I do not feel the pain they say is in your heart."

"So the crocodile ... somehow her human must've been close to me?"

Mushookie nodded and then added, "We younger creatures ... the ones who were forgotten *after* the Great Battle, we don't really see the fight the older creatures are struggling against about whether or not you should remember your old world. The older creatures who do not feel the pain do not see why it would be best for you to go back and I think they fear that if you went back, the shadowy creatures would return."

I pondered this and then inquired, "What do you think? Who are you siding with?"

We were out of the forest now and walking through the meadows. Mushookie answered, "Like I said before, I am young and do not see what the fuss is all about. I am neutral, either way. My human never knew you, so I cannot feel the pain Lucky does."

I shook my head, "Maybe you don't feel the pain, but surely you know about the battle with the shadowy creatures and how I needed to be here to stop them from destroying all. Do you fear the shadowy creatures will return if I leave?"

Mushookie thought a while, but finally said, "Nay, I do not fear the past. What is to be done will be done. You are the Dove of Light's golden keeper; if you are to return to your old home, then He will allow it to happen. He will know if the shadowy creatures will return if you leave. Please try to understand—the Dove of Light does what He thinks is best."

I nodded and stated, "I think I do understand. I just wish I knew what I had to remember to ease Lucky's suffering. I believe he feels the pain the most. All I know is that I should remember a certain boy and a certain name."

Mushookie shrugged and then his ears shot upright as he said, "Lucky is coming back; I hear him. I think I shall leave now. I only stayed to keep you from getting lonely. Good day to you, Queen Zora."

With that, Mushookie turned away from me and bounded over the grassy hills. Minutes after he disappeared, Lucky appeared at my side, a frustrated look was on his face. I touched his head with my hand and asked, "Where have you been? And why do you seem angry?"

Lucky looked up at me and sighed, "I was talking with Emily. I was trying to get her to tell me how to send you back. All she said though was: 'The answer lies within the castle.' What the heck is that supposed to mean?"

I shrugged and said, "Let's go back to the castle then. Maybe we need to be inside to find the answer."

Lucky agreed to my idea and we began walking back to the castle. As we walked, Lucky said, "I assume you believe that you came from a different world now?"

I nodded and added, "I'm not dead, Lucky. I learned that you and I are stuck in this waiting room. We are trapped somewhere in between two worlds."

Lucky was quiet for a while, but then said solemnly, "Aye. So you know the importance of this place then. It is not a bad place, infact it is most wonderful, but you wanted true love so badly, and I … I robbed you of it. I, perhaps, am a lousy friend."

I retorted harshly, "Lucky! That is enough nonsense from you! I am starting to agree with Conrad in that a heart is a very troublesome thing."

Lucky replied indifferently, "The heart is a troubling thing, Zora, but it makes you who you are."

We walked in silence then, until we got to the castle. When I entered through the doors, I noticed for the first time that there were many doors that I had not yet opened and looked through. Lucky noticed me examining the doors and he said, "You never noticed any of them except for your bedroom and the bathroom because you were always more excited to explore the land than what was inside a stuffy, old building."

I walked over to a green door—the one that had been in Conrad's memories and rested my hand on the doorknob. Lucky sighed sadly, "Ah, so you know that is the door that I came through then, but Alas! *You* cannot go through it to your world. Open it and see for yourself."

I opened the door and saw the same blue sky that had been in Conrad's memories. Lucky gazed at the vast emptiness as well and murmured, "We cannot go through it, for we are both here. No one is calling us back, and if someone from your world did want you back, they would not know what words to use to call you. I'm sure people are still crying over your disappearance, but they knew you had to go."

I put my hand through the door, but nothing felt different. I waved my hand through the air on the other side of the door, and when I looked down, I only saw more blue. I stepped out with one foot hesitantly, and placed it on an invisible surface in the blue sky. Then I stepped through the door, and both of my feet were on the surface of the invisible floor. I turned around and looked at Lucky questioningly. He tilted his head to one side and said, "You may have been able to walk through the door, but all you'll be able to do is wander through an empty sky. Come back through here, Zora, for if you start walking around in there, I will have no choice but to follow you and that room is boring. It's not going to get us anywhere anyways. Maybe one of the other rooms ..."

I walked back out of the blue room and into the castle again and then went to the next door. This door was pink with red roses painted on it. The green stems and leaves of the roses twined around the door beautifully. I looked at Lucky and he nodded at me to proceed with opening the door.

I slowly opened the door and a golden ray of light washed over us. When Lucky and I looked in the room, Lucky gasped in astonishment. In the room was a single glass table, and on the table, there was a strange book and a pen. I walked over to the table and Lucky followed me. I looked at the book and saw that it was green with the word "Diary" scribbled across the front in gold.

Lucky stood up on his hind legs and put his front paws on the table as he sniffed the diary. He looked at me, his face of pure shock and he stammered, "Zora, this ... this is your diary from your world. You wrote in it quite a bit, I remember well. You wrote about your emotions here. I have never been in this room before because I was always with you and you did not care about these rooms inside this castle. But I wonder how it got here."

I put my hand on the diary and traced the gold letters with my index finger. Then I carefully picked it up and opened the cover. The pages cracked as I leafed through them, and Lucky sighed, "Ah, the Land of Inspiration has made the book appear old so you would not make anything of it, had you ever chanced upon this room. But then why is it here? Perhaps the Dove of Light wants you to return your world. I am not sure though, His intentions are always so unclear until the time is right. He works in mysterious ways."

I looked down to read the words scribbled on the pages, but before I could, Lucky suddenly snatched it from me. He dropped the book on the ground and placed a paw over it as he explained hastily, "I forgot Zora. I am sorry I had to take it from you, but I can't let you read it until you tell me the boy's name. Do you even have the slightest clue yet?"

I shook my head and let my eyes rest on the diary ... my diary. I murmured, as if in a trance by the diary, "But Lucky, maybe if I read the name, maybe then I would remember."

Lucky shook his head and his fur stood on end as he growled, "No Zora. Your brother's name did not mean anything to you, so why would this other boy's? No. I will not let you read it."

I crossed my arms and huffed. Lucky's expression softened and he stated, "Come Zora, don't be difficult. Let's go to the next room, yes?"

I nodded reluctantly and we exited the room. I looked across the hall where three more doors stood, directly across from the three rooms we had already looked through. But as I made my way to a dark blue door with yellow stars painted upon it, a creature suddenly jumped in front of me and called out in a gruff voice, "Wait Queen Zora! Don't go in that room! You are not ready for that room yet!"

I jumped back and looked at the creature with a perplexed stare. Lucky was growling softly behind me, but he seemed rather frightened by the strange creature's enormous size. The creature had two white, sharp curved horns on its head and had large brown eyes. He towered three heads above me and had shaggy brown fur, which made him appear bulkier than what he really was. His cloven hooves were white as was his shaggy beard on his chin. Had it not been for the tiny white wings on his back, I would have considered him to be an unusually large mountain goat.

When I did not say anything, the creature went on, "I am Silvershoes and I have been around this castle ever since you arrived here, Queen Zora. I am the boy's guardian, and it is not time for you to see him yet. You have not learned all that there is to be learned."

"What are you talking about?" I asked.

Silvershoes looked at Lucky with his great brown eyes and replied, "Lucky knows the boy of whom I speak of. The boy whom I watch over is the one who you desired for most when you were in your world. The Dove of Light has told me to watch over this door until it is time— it is not yet time."

Lucky didn't move, but stopped growling and stared at Silvershoes in disbelief. Silvershoes smiled at Lucky and stated gently, "Well my friend … I see you are learning and that you have come a few steps closer to restoring Zora's heart. It is a good thing too, for she has been here for two years already and my boy is beginning to think the events that happened that day weren't real. You have little time to spare, because when she enters the door where the creature Gooba lives, years will pass in her old world before she will be done with what he has to tell her. Time travels quickly behind the door next to this one that I guard, so make haste! What you find may startle you, but you must not let it frighten you so much that you forget why you are there. Good luck my friends, and hurry!"

I at once began to move towards the door next to the blue one with the yellow stars, and I saw that it was a door that was half black and half white. The doorknob on it was glowing brightly, and I wondered how I had ever missed seeing it before. Although Silvershoes had a very commanding voice, Lucky did not at once follow me, but he stood glaring at Silvershoes for a long time and asked bitterly, "Why have you not shown yourself to us before? Zora needs that heart piece back, and I know you feel the same pain I have felt for as long as I've been here because your boy loved Zora. Why did you wait … why did you live with the pain if you knew Zora had to only look among these doors and the pain would be cured? Now we all have to wait a little longer."

Silvershoes looked at Lucky with sadness in his eyes, and he murmured, "The Dove of Light had commanded me so. I could not disobey, and the Dove of Light, well … He always knows what's best. He has a reason for everything. Surely you must know this Lucky? Besides, the Dove of Light would not let the keeper of the Golden Happiness be sad or be left broken. Have faith, my friend!"

Lucky was humbled then and said respectfully, "Of course … the Dove of Light has a reason for everything. Thank you for reminding me dear friend, and I hope your boy will still love Zora, even when many years have past. I hope his memory, at least, is not broken. Off we go then, and I shall see you again when we come back out from this mysterious room."

Lucky then pattered after me, and I opened the door, and we were met with a fragrance of flowers. Though the room smelled heavenly, it was dark and somewhat gloomy, and I wondered why it was here on the Land of Inspiration. The room had crumbling gray bricks for walls, and the floor was cold soil. Cobwebs hung in the corner. Lucky and I cautiously stepped into the room, and the door slammed quickly behind us, and we jumped. We were at once in a room of darkness, and I began to tremble in fear, and I whispered to Lucky, "This room is scary, and I can't stop shaking."

A grouchy voice suddenly shouted out, "Aye it is dark! But I don't think it's scary, but rather just boring, but Alas! I know everything there is to know, and need not learn anything more. So I stay put."

I squinted through the dark, but couldn't see the source of the voice. Next to me, Lucky was growling softly. The voice spoke again. "Well, and I suppose I will have to light a candle and let some light fill this dim room before you speak, aye?"

I didn't respond, but suddenly, there was a sharp pop and then there was a flame in front of me on a candle that was resting in a holder on the ground. By the light that was cast, I could make out a smooth flat rock with moss on it, and standing on top of the rock was a strange creature. He had brown fur with a layer of thick off-white fur starting at his chin and going to the center of his chest, like a sort of beard. He had black round ears and long whiskers on his long, narrow snout. He had tiny red horns protruding from his head and also snowy white wings on his back. And then I saw his tail, and I began to wonder what this creature was, for his tail was like the form of the cloud in Conrad's memories. It was dark and billowy, and it seemed to me like the creature should belong in the Sea of Interference, for the billowy tail was frightful.

The creature stared at me with sharp, gray eyes and then he turned his head, as if to examine me with only one eye, and he crossed his arms across his chest and he huffed, "Well? Zora, what is it you wish of me? Obviously you have come here for answers and answers I will give you … But! Do not ask a question unless you are prepared for the answer!"

Lucky stepped forward before I could say anything and inquired, "And are you the Gooba that Silvershoes speaks of?"

The creature looked at Lucky, a haughty look in his eyes and I saw sharp teeth when he replied, "Well, and I am Gooba, but whether or not Silvershoes speaks of me … most would not know the answer to that question, for there may be more than one Gooba in this great land, but since I know everything, the answer to your question would have to be yes."

Gooba turned to look at me then and said, in his still grouchy voice, "And before you start questioning my knowledge, I will tell you this: I know you are here to find out how to get your memory back, and I know the good and bad outcomes of this getting your memory back nonsense, for I have been in the Sea of Interference and that is how I got this billowy, dark tail, and these demon horns. I am good though, and I am honest, so that is why I have angel's wings and a definite form like a creature from the Land of Inspiration."

I stood staring at him, looking stupefied, because by the sound of his voice, I could tell he knew that his shadowy tail made me uneasy. His arms were still crossed and he sat staring at me, his eyes penetrating my own, and finally I was able to ask, "Who created you then? You say you can answer any question, so how about that one— who's guardian are you?"

Gooba looked to the side again, and I saw a tear trickle down his cheek, but he swiftly wiped it away and then crossed his arms again and muttered, "I am no one's guardian … the Dove of Light and the Serpent of Darkness … they created me. The Dove of Light gave me the goodness, honesty, and definite form and the Serpent of Darkness gave me this billowy tail and the knowledge of consequences and doubt of all actions. Because of this sorrow that I can accidentally cause, the Dove of Light has kept me locked away in this room, and only He, the Serpent, and you can enter here. The guardians all know of me, and they are curious enough to want to ask me questions, but the Dove of Light knows that great evil could come from this constant questioning, and so he forbade them to enter, and has sealed this door shut. Lucky is able to come with you of course, because he is your guardian, and he plays a major role in what is to happen to you Zora. When the shadowy creatures attacked this land, I was still in here, and the Serpent could not paralyze me, for he is part of me."

Lucky then asked, "Well—you must know why we are here then, so tell us, can Zora get her memory and return to her old world without the shadowy creatures coming back?"

Gooba turned his head to look at us both with both eyes again and he grumbled, "Yes—she can both regain her memory and return to her old world without fear of the shadowy creatures from the Sea of Interference returning. But! Don't rejoice just yet about hearing this news, for when Zora finally remembers, she will have to make a difficult choice. The world from which she came from is not as carefree as this one, and when she returns, she will have no job and no home and no way to earn a living. Her parents will most likely allow her to stay with them for a little while, but then they will expect her to find a job to earn a living, but Zora will not easily adjust to this hard living, and sadness may overcome her. Being that she is the Dove of Light's chosen one, she will have chances to come back, but if she chooses to stay in this land after she has left and seen the boy again, her heart will always be aching. Zora cannot have both true love and a carefree life as she does in the Land of Inspiration."

Lucky looked up at me and I saw a deep sadness in his eyes and then I asked Gooba, "Can you feel the brokenness inside me, Gooba? Would you want me to remember my past life?"

Gooba answered swiftly, "I can feel your brokenness, but not because I am close to you like Lucky or some of the other guardians, but because I know everything. As for you remembering your past life … well, there are good and bad outcomes to remembering and not remembering. They are equal in consequences, so you must decide, not me."

I pondered this as Lucky asked, "So how do we get Zora to remember again?"

Gooba glared at Lucky and retorted, "*I* won't be doing anything— all I can do is tell you how you can go about getting her to remember. You are her guardian, so you must decide what you think is best for her. In the room next to this one, awaits the great Dove of Light. He has been waiting for you two for a while, but that does not mean He has forgotten His obligations and duties. He still is giving guardian airs to newborns and keeping watch over this land, but He is able to do it from His room until you come to visit Him and He has told you what you need to do. He has made it, though, so that you had to visit me first so I can tell you what problems may come about when you finally re-member.

"The first thing is that you will only be able to visit your world when it is dark on the boy's half of the world ... until you've made your decision that is. The decision that you must make is whether you want true love more, or to live in a world with absolutely no problems. You'll have to make a decision whether you want the boy more, or this world. You'll understand what I'm talking about better after you've been to your world again. Also, since Lucky has already been seen in your old world in flesh and blood, he will be like an ordinary dog once you return ... at least to those who have seen the Serpent. So, you will have to live with that sort of commotion in your life, for people *will* talk to you about it. I would suggest living someplace secluded to avoid all this ... maybe even change your name."

"Change my name, but—," I began, but Gooba cut me off with a glare and then he looked at Lucky and another big tear rolled down his cheek as he stated with a touch of pity, "And if Zora does decide to stay, there is a big risk that you may be forgotten, Lucky."

Lucky jumped forward at once and cried out angrily, "What?! Why? That can't be—you must be lying—Zora would *never* forget me!"

I nodded in agreement, and although I seethed inside with the same anger Lucky was feeling, I held my tongue, for Gooba suddenly jumped down from his rock and shook an accusing finger at Lucky as he retorted, "Now just you listen to me! I can never lie—the Dove of Light makes me to be honest with everyone, and I would not have shown you so much pity had I not felt the pain you feel. I'm sorry, Lucky, guardian of Zora, but you cannot stop fate from happening."

Gooba jumped back on his rock and crossed his arms again, facing us, as Lucky stood staring at him, mouth open. Gooba glanced at me and then looked back at Lucky as he said, more subtle now, "Lucky—remember how weak Zora's mind was when she was infatuated with him? How you could sometimes not get through to her and how you were barely hanging on to her by a thread? All I'm saying is that to give Zora what she wants most, you may have to let her go. All humans forget their guardians eventually, Lucky; either through lack of imagination or being too preoccupied with their lives or love ... Zora was a special case because she was the keeper of the Golden

Happiness. If she decides to stay in her old world, the Dove of Light will have to take that power away because since she has been in the Land of Inspiration, the power has made her immortal. She can't be immortal in her old world—can you imagine how painful that would be? To see all your loved ones die, while you continue to show no signs of age?"

Lucky shook his head, not believing, and I myself was numb by the knowledge of this creature. Lucky stammered, "H-how? How can He take the power away? Doesn't it need to stay inside Zora?"

Gooba shook his head and replied, "If the Dove of Light can give her the power, He can take it away as well. The Golden Happiness had to be in her world in order to grow and be of any use against the shadowy creatures. Now, however, the power that Zora has nurtured is so strong, we need not fear of the creatures from the Sea of Interference any more. Doubt, of course, will always be present in human life, but the Serpent of Darkness's evil plan of submerging the world in complete unhappiness will never be pursued again, and the shadowy creatures will never be able to enter this land again. If the Dove of Light takes the power from Zora, He will just keep it here in this land—it won't disappear like many creatures here think it will. Basically what I'm trying to say is that whatever Zora chooses, it won't affect this land or her world in any major way. Only her friends and family will be affected by her choice, for they love her, but the world outside her life won't be any different than it is now."

There was a long silence then, until Lucky questioned, "What about the boy then? Will he love Zora if she returns? She was always quiet, but—"

"Shush puppy," Gooba interrupted, "The boy was never more attracted to her than that last day when she showed her admiration for him. Of course, since by the time Zora goes back, eight years will have passed in that world, and the boy may need a little refreshing of his mind. Time can heal anything, but you will have to approach him with gentleness and caution, for he believes Zora is gone forever. As time can heal Zora's relationship with him, time has also been healing his longing for her, and so he's … well, let's just put it this way—he loved her, but that's not going to stop him from loving others. He didn't get to know her well enough. All he really knew was that she cared enough for him to sacrifice everything she had."

Lucky was quiet for a long time again, but finally he asked, "Will … will they be happy together though? Will Zora eventually adjust to the ways of her own world if she chooses the boy?"

Gooba nodded and sighed, as if with a sudden twinge of passion, "Ah—true love the two sweet things will find in each other, and they will both be healed. The boy is already living what most people would consider a successful life in his world, and so he can surely help Zora to adjust … though it won't be easy. The boy is not considered *rich* in his world, but he is certainly not poor either, but Zora is used to a rich person's life, since her memory of a normal life has been erased. Then again, the Dove of Light will help her to remember, hopefully, before she goes, but still … things will be unclear to her."

Lucky and I pondered all that this creature had told us, and suddenly I inquired, "Gooba? Before I came here, I saw a crocodile with six legs, and she felt the pain that Lucky did. Her human had died and I saw a light join with the crocodile and then they went up to the great Sun of Happiness. I was just wondering … who was the human, and how did I know them when I was in my old world?"

Gooba pulled on his ears and moaned, "Oh poor Zora! But I suppose you will have to learn sooner or later, but the man was your great grandfather. Of course this won't mean anything until the Dove of Light helps you to recover bits of your memory. Now … you must go, for much time has passed in your old world. You must return to the boy if you wish to be happy with him."

I turned to leave, but Lucky shouted, "Wait! Gooba, I have one more question: What do you think Zora should do?"

Gooba turned his back to us and his ears drooped as he replied somberly, "I'm sorry my friend, but I have no opinions of my own. I … I am not allowed to decide the fate of others, though I already know the outcome … oh! Just go to the Dove of Light now, will you?! You are wasting precious time here—*go!*"

The door suddenly whooshed open and a cold rush of air came in and blew out the candle, and even though I could no longer see him, I knew Gooba was glaring at us, and by no doubt, another tear was trickling down his cheek. Lucky and I exited the room and Silvershoes greeted us with curious eyes and he asked, "Well? How did it go? Do you have your memory back, Zora?"

I shook my head and silently went to a yellow door with a big orange sun painted on it as Lucky explained to Silvershoes, "We must see the Dove of Light first. Silvershoes, for the sake of my girl, I hope your boy will still remember and love."

Silvershoes nodded and agreed, "As do I. Keep your hopes up friend, for it was not my boy whose memory was erased by us, and certainly by seeing her again, his old admiration for her will be aroused."

I opened the door and a ray of warm, golden sunshine met me. Lucky was behind me in seconds and he murmured in awe, "It is He, Zora. It's Him!"

I glanced over at Silvershoes and he gave me a hopeful and encouraging look, and I stepped into the room with Lucky at my heels. The door closed lightly behind us, and I looked past the golden glow and saw a large snow white dove. He looked at me with gentle eyes and His voice was pleasant, yet it had an air of authority when He said, "Good day to you Zora. I have been waiting here for you for a long time … although I knew you'd find me eventually. The creatures here may have been able to take away your memory, but they can't take away your curiosity or who you really are."

I was stunned in awe by His magnificence and I couldn't speak, for I was lost for words, but Lucky was ready for answers and a cure, and he hastily asked, "Well, great Dove of Light, Gooba told us you can restore Zora's memory and then she can go back to the boy and restore her heart piece. Can you really do this?"

The Dove of Light turned His gentle eyes to Lucky and replied, "Yes, I can do that. Do you doubt my powers, Lucky, Guardian of Zora?"

Lucky hesitated and then murmured, "No … I just don't see the reason behind your actions. Why would you allow the guardians to take away her memory and then make her suffer through a broken heart? Even though she can't feel it, I can, and I know it's hurting her."

The Dove of Light replied simply, "I needed to give her time to recover and I needed to find out if the boy would love her if she went back. I consulted Gooba, for he knows the good and the bad. He scoffed at me saying, 'You gave the humans guardians. Why not ask them? They would know.' I told him then that yes I indeed gave the humans guardians, but how would they know the future? I also pointed out that when the Dark Serpent and I created him, I lost my power to see what the future held for the humans." The Dove of Light said this last part with a twinge of sadness and regret.

I asked quietly, "Why did you create Gooba then? Didn't you know you would lose your power?"

The Dove of Light nodded and explained, "I had the power before I created Gooba, and the Serpent had a similar power that he lost in Gooba's creation as well. I decided to create Gooba because the Serpent sometimes corrupted the humans, and those who forget their guardians and imagination and ignore their conscience are lost forever in a never ending sea of darkness, but they don't feel it for their souls are lost. I would rather not know which humans were going to be saved and which ones were going to be lost until the final day has come for them, for then I know. I can still feel when humans doubt, and I try to get through to them, and I never give up or are tempted to give up because I'll never know what is to become of them. I could always ask Gooba, but I think it is better that I don't. I … I sometimes feel sorry for the burden I cast on Gooba, but the Serpent lost his future sightseeing abilities as well, and so long as he doesn't know which humans are the easiest to attack, well … things are just better this way. I lost some of my power, but so did the Serpent, so it was for the best.

"The Serpent likes to make life miserable for humans. He feeds off negative thoughts and sorrow, and his shadows settle in with the humans like a guardian might, but instead of encouraging them, they persuade the humans they torment that life is horrible. In the end though, all humans have a chance to enter the Sun of Happiness if they are willing."

Lucky asked, "So where do I and all the other guardians come into play then? Explain that to Zora."

"Well, each guardian is made up of guardian airs, or a conscience, that I give to each person that is born. When the person is around three to five, they give the guardian a shape and they are most commonly known as imaginary friends. When the child gets too bored of an imaginary friend or someone tells them they are too old for one, the guardian comes here to the Land of Inspiration where they can still be connected to their human and guide them through life, but when they are here, they are more faint. When the human dies, they come here first, reunite with their guardian, and then go up to the Sun of Happiness."

"What about the people who have two guardians? How is that possible, and are those people any different from anyone else?" I asked.

The Dove of Light shook his head and answered, "The number of imaginary friends is limitless. You had other imaginary friends beside Lucky when you were little, but Lucky was your conscience because you thought of him the most and before the others. You had always wanted a golden retriever when you were younger and that's how your guardian came to be. People who appear to have two guardians or consciences are just the people who thought of two imaginary friends at the same time and spent equal attention to them both, but they are no different than anyone else. What your guardian looks like alone, does not determine the amount of creativity one has, but rather it comes from a variety of things, like if you are always thinking of new games or new ideas."

There was a long moment of silence as I thought about all that the Dove of Light had told me. Finally, I murmured, "Good Dove? I hear I have a brother, and it saddens me that I can't remember him. Can you make me remember him again … please?"

The Dove of Light smiled, blinked, and then suddenly there was a sharp pop and my diary appeared in front of the Dove of Light. Then, as if by some magical force, the pages began to turn and when they stopped, the Dove of Light looked down at the page and instructed, "If you wish to remember your brother, then listen to what I have to say, Zora. This is but one memory of your brother that you had written, but after I read just one, others will also be unburied. This is one thing that you wrote:

'Today Bradley had his graduation party. He didn't want one, but mom and dad kind of forced him into it. I think it's good that he has a party—it's a one in a lifetime deal. If he didn't have one, he would probably regret it later on in life. A lot of people showed up, which I think Bradley kind of disliked. He wasn't really looking forward to going around and talking to everyone, but grandma says it's good for him. I guess she's right. It's kind of sad to see him done with school— it's almost like he's leaving childhood forever, but I guess the memories we share will always be present. It's not like he's going to

disappear forever ... even though he talks about moving out of state sometimes.'"

The Dove of Light stopped and looked at me, and then He quickly fanned out His wings and suddenly, a wave of memories washed over me. Bradley, my brother, was abruptly brought back to me, and I saw him with his wavy, short, dusty-brown hair and his dark brown eyes. I heard his laughter even, and his voice as I listened to him tell me his most present dream, but these were only memories. I fell to my knees as I began to remember my other family members as well; my aunts and uncles, my cousins and grandparents, and finally, my mom and dad. Tears began to swell in my eyes, and I saw Lucky's mouth fall open. He knew I remembered again.

I looked at the Dove of Light and whispered hoarsely, "I ... I can't believe I ... I forgot them. Tell me more please .... tell me about the boy Lucky wants me so desperately to remember. Read me a page about him please."

The Dove of Light gave me an encouraging smile and replied, "Of course, little one. Here is a small thing you wrote about the boy you were infatuated with:

'Grr, I wish my heart were not so troublesome! I wish I would not fall in love so easily. I want to talk to him, but I can't! My brain slows down and I can't think because I think he's so perfect. Maybe at the next dance, I can ask him to dance with me. Oh! But courage must find me first!'"

The Dove of Light paused and then continued, "You did dance with the boy, Zora. Here is what you wrote after the dance:

'I can't believe it! I actually had the courage to ask him. I asked him to dance with me, and he said yes! We talked about our love for running and how people thought we were crazy. But I can't let myself think anything of it—it was one dance ... nothing more.'"

The Dove of Light stopped and flapped His wings again and more memories flooded my conscience. It was overwhelming almost and I saw the boy of my dreams again, and I gasped, "Oh! Denver Trievus! It was Denver ... I ..."

I broke off and buried my face into my hands and wept as memories of my other friends were also brought back. As the tears rolled steadily down my cheeks, I sobbed, "Oh Lucky! How ... how could I have forgotten them?! My family and my friends! They had always meant so much to me, and I forgot them. What happened to me?"

Lucky was at my side in seconds and was soothing, "Shush now Zora, and do not cry! You have finally remembered what I wanted you to. I can feel the darkness that filled the hole that you had in your heart start to fade away. You're going to be healed little one, so be merry!"

I continued to sob though and my shoulders shook, and then suddenly the Dove of Light flew to me and embraced me in His soft, white wings and He said, "Now, now Zora. Everything is going to be okay. You must trust me though and trust that I know what I am doing. Stop crying now little one, and say you trust me."

I was comforted by His strong, soothing voice and I stopped crying. He let me go and stood back a little and I looked up at Him and said, "Okay. I promise I'll trust that you know what you're doing. I trust you."

The Dove of Light nodded and His smile deepened and then He continued, "Good girl." He paused and then added quietly, "That dance … it was Senior Prom dance … a few days before graduation. You were always quiet, and you always thought showing love for someone was a sort of weakness. That's why it took you so long to get the courage to ask. Plus, you were afraid of rejection, but afterwards, well … never mind. You will find out for yourself what Denver thought of you. He never knew you had liked him because you were so subtle in your actions, but forget what I say now. It is time for you to visit him."

I looked up at him and trembled as I inquired, "You mean I visit Denver? But how?"

The Dove of Light answered, "When you leave this room, Silvershoes will allow you to enter through the blue door with the yellow stars on it, and that will take you to Denver's yard, but you will arrive there at night time."

I protested, "At night time?! You must be crazy; he'll call the cops! He probably thinks I'm dead anyways."

The Dove of Light shook His head and replied, "No, He won't call the cops. Lucky will be with you, and he will find the spare key that Denver keeps in his backyard. You will be able to let yourself in, and then you must let Lucky wake him and you must stay hidden until Lucky explains things. Hopefully, Denver will remember Lucky. And he knows you are not dead, for he saw what happened the last day.

Now, no more arguing—you must go now before more time passes. Go—and good luck!"

Before I had time to ask anything else, the wind suddenly got stronger and pushed us out of the room, and we were in the hallway of the castle once more. The door of the room we just came out of had closed again and I looked at it, helplessly and still confused.

Silvershoes came over to us at once and exclaimed, "Zora! I feel a change in you! You are remembering again and the Dove of Light has returned to the big sun, for I do not feel His presence in that room anymore. Now, you must go through this door, and when the sun comes up in Denver's world, you will come back here. Some crazy rule of Gooba's I think, but hurry now! Much time has been wasted already. Go now, for it is night time there at this moment—hurry!"

I didn't have time to object, for Lucky was pulling at my dress with his teeth and leading me to the door with the yellow stars, and Silvershoes was pushing me from behind.

The door flew open and I saw a black sky, and I was frightened at first, but then I saw a small white light in the black darkness. It gradually grew bigger and bigger until suddenly, Silvershoes shoved both Lucky and me through the door. A cold air rushed by me and I felt like I was falling. I grabbed for Lucky and held him securely in my arms and closed my eyes tightly. From above, Silvershoes cried out, "Hurry Zora! But don't mess this up or you'll both be crushed! Speak gently with him!"

Wind rushed up from below and I screamed as I felt my stomach lurch, and then suddenly, I felt my feet on something wet and cold, but soft. I abruptly stopped screaming. I opened my eyes and set Lucky down on the grass and then I looked at my surroundings.

Chapter 7

Zora

We were suddenly standing in a dark yard—Lucky and I. The grass was cool and moist on my bare feet and I shivered. The sun being gone was something new for me, but a bright moon overhead lit up the sky and the trees cast perfect shadows on the ground.

Lucky looked at me and then he followed my gaze to a small white house that set on the tidy yard. There were green shutters on the windows and there was a beautiful oak door. Lucky asked, "Well Zora? Are you going to go in? You only have until the sun comes up."

I hesitated and stammered, "But Lucky … isn't this a bit awkward? And how am I supposed to get in? If he's anything like I remember before you came and took me away … well … I probably won't be welcomed."

Lucky shook his head and said, "You still aren't remembering the last few hours that you were here before I swept you away to the Land of Inspiration. In that little time that you had to choose between the ends of the earth or your most wanted desire, he seemed to respect you. You'll never know unless you talk to him."

I took a few steps forward, and then stopped. I stared at the door, suddenly very afraid of it. Lucky urged, "Come now Zora, don't back down now. You've already come this far."

I finished walking to the door and rested my hand on the doorknob. My voice trembled as I asked quietly, "But how am I to get in Lucky?

The door is locked and what if I startle him? I don't think this is a good idea ... especially at night. It's kind of creepy actually."

Lucky gave me a stern look, but replied calmly, "The Dove of Light said there was a spare key around here, remember? And The Dove of Light is watching you. He cannot control what happens next, but if this does not go well, He will take you from here and banish all thoughts of Denver from your mind and make sure you never remember him again so he can't cause you any trouble or pain. You'll be fine, trust me. I'm your guardian and I won't let anything bad happen to you. Any rough spots we'll get through, I'm sure."

I crossed my arms and looked up at the bright moon, pondering how to respond, but Lucky gave me no time and merely said, "I'll go get that key then. You're going to go in and you're going to have a lovely talk with Denver Trievus. Understand?"

I opened my mouth to protest, but he silenced me with a firm look and began sniffing the doorknob. After a while, he stepped back and pointed his nose towards the air and began sniffing some more. Finally, he must've got the right scent, because his ears perked up and he trotted to the back of the house. When he came back, he was holding his head high and he had a smug look on his face. In his mouth dangled the keys.

Lucky dropped the keys at my feet and I hastily bent to pick them up. Lucky's eyes sparkled and he laughed at my eagerness and said quietly, "You see? You do want to see Denver again. You just need the courage ... that's why I'm here for you—to make sure you don't back down."

I put the key into the door and unlocked it, but then I hesitated again. "Lucky," I said, "What if ..." I flushed, but continued on in a murmur, "What if Denver is married? What if ...?"

I trailed off, but Lucky said sternly, "Zora. If Denver was married, do you think the Dove of Light would've let you come back? Do you think He would've let us creatures help you to remember your past life just so you could be disappointed? Maybe He doesn't know how Denver's future is going to play out, but He is able to go to Gooba anytime He wishes and ask. And besides, The Dove of Light is watching you through me. The Dove of Light loves you Zora—you're the chosen one!"

I took a deep breath and then as quietly as I could, I opened the door. The room inside was dark, for all the lights were off. Lucky whispered, "Put your hand on my head and I will lead you to him. Walk carefully though, and tread quietly."

I rested my hand on Lucky's head as he instructed and we began to walk through the house. We hadn't gone but a few feet before I stumbled over a pair of shoes. I was able to keep myself from crying out, but the thud that I had made with my feet when I tried to catch myself seemed louder than ever in the dark silence of the room.

Lucky and I held our breaths and listened for any signs of movement, but we heard nothing except for the ticking of a clock in another room. We exhaled and I muttered quietly, "Shoes, Lucky! That's what I tripped on! But no surprise there really … he loved to run."

Lucky sniffed the shoes and then recoiled from them quickly and whispered, "And from the smells of things, I'd say he *still* loves running. I smell sweat mingling in with the many scents of mud and leaves and grass. These shoes have been on many trails."

I stifled a laugh and we continued through the house. Lucky led me up a flight of stairs, and soon we were standing in front of a door that was slightly open. We heard soft breathing coming from within and fear welled up inside of me again. Lucky felt my growing anxiety and licked my hand at once, urging me to go on. I knew he would stay with me no matter what, and that gave me courage, so I finally, slowly and quietly, opened the door.

I was relieved that the door didn't creak, for then I had time to examine my surroundings. It was still dark, but a window provided enough moonlight to seep in for me to make out the shapes of a dresser, a bed, and a lamp and alarm clock on an end table. The alarm clock gave me the time of 4:30 A.M. I only had faint memories of what time was, but I knew well enough that my presence around 4:30 in the morning would not be welcomed.

Lucky felt my thoughts at once and whispered, "Zora, why don't you walk over and see him? Quietly though, you don't want to start off on the wrong foot and startle him."

Without arguing, I walked on quiet feet over to the bed where a figure slept and from where the breathing noises were coming from. My heart skipped a beat and I seemed to stop breathing when I saw his face. Sure, I had faintly remembered bits and pieces of his features when the Dove of Light brought forth my memories, but they were imperfect memories before. Now, everything seemed to fall into place. I started to remember huge chunks of my past life. There were so many memories that I almost burst from the force at which they came tumbling back into view. Birthday parties and sleepovers with my friends and family, the many talks I had with my friends about our boy troubles, the pets that I had, and the house and fields and trees surrounding it that had once been my home.

I looked at Denver Trievus and saw his short, tousled brown hair atop his still boyish face. But he wasn't a boy anymore—how many years had passed since the last day of high school? Gooba had told me eight years would have passed before I finally made my way back to my old world ... my home. I calculated the years in my head and came to the answer that Denver was twenty-five or twenty-six years old ... but I was trapped at eighteen until I made up my mind of whether to stay or not.

I reached out my hand to touch his soft face, but I withdrew quickly, remembering that the Dove of Light had said that Lucky was to wake him. I cast another quick glance at his face—at his closed eyes, remembering that they were a most captivating blue when opened—and then walked away towards the window. Lucky followed me and asked quietly, "Well? Shall I wake him then Zora, so that you may talk with him? It's now or never, but I want to do what you wish. If you are not ready we can always come back later, but who knows how long it will be. Do you really want to wait any longer?"

I hesitated and rubbed my arm uncomfortably. I was shaking too and my heart was pounding, but I murmured, "You're right, Lucky, it's now or never ... but gosh this is so awkward, and ... and *weird*. But I suppose I don't want any more time to pass than what has already. I've got to know. Go ahead."

Lucky nodded and smiled. Then he turned back towards the bed and trotted over to it. He put his front paws on the bed and barked softly. Denver merely turned away from him, still asleep. Lucky whimpered and then tugged gently on Denver's shirt with his teeth. Denver merely pushed Lucky away and muttered, "Go away Otto, I'm trying to sleep."

Lucky looked at me and smiled smugly as he stated, "He must have a dog. This is going to be easier than I thought."

Before I could ask what he meant, he stood back a little ways from the bed and started to bark really loud. Another bark from somewhere in the house answered, and fear overwhelmed me again. What if this other dog wasn't friendly? I had no time to run out of the house though, because at that moment, Denver's eyes popped opened and when he saw Lucky, he jumped out of bed and muttered, "What the he—,"

Another smaller dog burst into the room at that moment, cutting off Denver's curse. This dog was a small black and brown long-haired thing and I laughed quietly in spite of myself for being scared of it before I saw it. Denver did not hear me however, for the smaller dog and Lucky were both barking, and suddenly a cloud covered the moon, and my presence was concealed by darkness, but I could still make out the shapes of the figures in the room.

In the dark, I heard the small dog yipping at Lucky, but then Lucky growled and scolded sharply, "Now shame on you! Such a puny thing you are and growling at a guardian from the Land of Inspiration! Shush now! Bad dog—and go away!"

The dog was instantly silenced, alarmed at the fact that Lucky was scolding it as a human would, and Denver looked equally perplexed. He backed away from Lucky and when Lucky saw this movement, he asked bitterly, "Now is that the way you're supposed to treat an old friend? Denny-boy, are you getting forgetful?"

There was silence and then I heard Denver's voice saying, "That voice … I remember it from somewhere, but I can't place it. No wait. Dogs can't talk … this must be a dream. That's the only explanation."

The clouds moved a bit from the moon, and enough light seeped in so that I could see Lucky suddenly lunging towards Denver and ripping off the white t-shirt that he wore. Denver tried swatting at Lucky, but he stepped back quickly and dropped the mangled shirt on the floor.

Denver yelled, "Hey, you dumb mutt! You destroyed my shirt!"

Lucky retorted, "I am no mutt, you fool! I am a purebred golden retriever, for that is what Zora wished me to be when she created me out of the guardian airs the Dove of Light gave to her."

The clouds moved once more away from the moon and the light was finally enough so that I could see the look of astonishment on Denver's face. He was looking at Lucky however and still hadn't noticed me. He questioned, "Zora? Is that what you just said? So then that means … you must be Lucky! I remember now."

Lucky sat on the floor, looking quite smug with how things were going, and he softened his voice towards Denver as he replied, "Yes, I did say the name Zora. And I am glad that you know who I am, for that will make things a lot quicker and easier."

Lucky paused and was about to continue, but Denver asked quickly, "Where is she then? You wouldn't be here if Zora wasn't somehow involved in this. It's been so long since I last saw her. You took her away before she graduated. I remember … she got her diploma, and then that black cloud—"

Lucky interrupted, "Yes, yes. I know all about that day. I am Zora's guardian and so I have been monitoring her every move. You have a guardian too … all humans do, but never mind that. Denny-boy, I am here to ask you a question. Would you like to see Zora again?"

I was surprised when Denver actually replied, "Of course! She saved my life, and I never really got a chance to thank her. Is she here … right now?"

Lucky lay down on the floor and yawned as if bored. He murmured monotonously, "I don't know. Look around; maybe she is here. I doubt it, I mean, you saw her leave and you knew she was never to come back, but if you really want to see her again, maybe she'll just suddenly appear out of nowhere."

All at once, the clouds completely moved away from the moon, and the light that shown in was very bright. Denver looked over to the window and saw me and exclaimed, "Zora! Lucky said you were going to be gone forever when he took you away, but you're back!"

I smiled uncertainly at him and began, "Well yeah … it's all very confusing actually. I'm not sure how I got back and I'm not even sure if I remember my whole life yet, but somehow I think …"

I trailed off, not really certain where I was going with this. I was so nervous and the silence was unbearable, but I didn't know what to say. I was at a loss for words when in his presence. Finally he asked, "Uh, Zora … how did you get inside my house? Was the door unlocked? Or did you just kind of appear here?"

He said the last part jokingly, but I was too nervous to even laugh. I stammered, "Well, um. Lucky … he kind of found your spare key. We were teleported from the Land of Inspiration to your yard and once we had the key … we let ourselves in and … please don't be mad. We could only come at night."

I wanted to run out of the room or hide in a hole or something, but Denver surprised me yet again by simply saying, "Oh. Well so long as you didn't break a window or something." I laughed nervously and he smiled as he noted, "You're wearing a crown. Are you some sort of princess now or something?"

My cheeks turned red, but fortunately it was dark enough so Denver couldn't see me. I had forgotten about the crown, but suddenly I felt its weight and presence again, and I remembered why I had it, and so I replied, my voice smoother, "No. I'm not a princess. I'm a queen."

Lucky interjected teasingly, "And best you not forget it Denny-boy."

Denver glanced at Lucky and then looked back at me and joked, "Oh, I'm sorry, your *highness*. Am I going to have to bow to you or something before you tell me where you've been and what's going on?"

I shook my head quickly and replied, "Oh no! I wouldn't make you do that! But I … I came to say I'm sorry."

Lucky even looked a little perplexed as Denver inquired, "You're sorry? What for?"

I hesitated, but then responded in a rush, "Um, for annoying you and waking you up at 4:30 in the morning. Well actually I mean I'm sorry for annoying you when we were in high school. You know how I talked to you all the time on the internet, but very little at school? I'm sure it annoyed you because it would have annoyed me … but I just found it so hard to talk to you."

Denver rubbed his eyes sleepily and murmured, "Zora, what are you talking about? You haven't annoyed me … well maybe a little in high school, but you saved my life."

I sighed in relief, and Lucky said, "See? I told you so, Zora."

I scowled at him, but then I turned back to Denver and asked curiously, "Why aren't you acting like this is all very strange? You're too calm. I don't understand it."

There was a brief moment of silence, but Denver finally replied, "Because this is a dream. It has to be. And even if it wasn't, I don't think I would be surprised, because after that last day you were here, nothing takes me by surprise anymore. It was all very strange."

I am dismayed by this news, and even Lucky was caught off guard by his response, for he jumped up quickly and cried out, "Denver! How can you possibly think that this is a dream?! We've been talking for nearly fifteen minutes now!" I glanced over the alarm clock and saw that Lucky spoke the truth, and then I was brought back to Lucky when he said to Denver, "You said you remembered me. I thought that meant you knew this wasn't a dream. This isn't a dream Denver Trievus. This is real!"

Denver walked over to his bed and sat down as he replied, "I'm not sure. Graduation … the sky turned black and Zora was sucked into it. How can she be standing in my room right now?"

He seemed to be talking to himself, for his voice was in a low murmur. Lucky looked at me and then muttered, "If I were you, I'd slap him right about now."

I certainly wasn't going to slap him, but I walked over to him and sat down on the bed next to him. I touched his shoulder hesitantly and when he looked up I asked, "What do I need to do to convince you that this is real? There must be something. I'm not an illusion … I'm really here."

Denver shrugged and I sighed heavily, feeling helpless. Lucky suddenly walked over to us and quickly bit Denver's leg. Denver yelped and pulled away swiftly, as I cried out at the same time, "Lucky!"

Lucky backed away, glaring at Denver, until Denver finally said, "All right, all right! This is real … but how?"

Lucky replied simply, "The Dove of Light, the creator of guardians. He needed Zora as a keeper of the golden light, but now that the task is done she can come back … if she chooses."

Denver looked back at me and asked, "Wait, so are you an angel then or something? Were you in heaven?"

I shook my head and replied, "I already told you I'm a queen. And I haven't been in heaven. I'm not sure what that even is, but I was stuck in the Land of Inspiration. That's a place for the guardians in between a place called the Sun of Happiness and Earth. The creatures there took away my memory when I arrived there, but the Dove of Light recently gave it back. But … I'm still missing some pieces of my memory. Like I don't remember graduation day, but I remember that that was the day

I was taken here and I know I was taken away because that was the only way I could protect you."

Denver placed his hand on my hand and when he looked up at me, he finally whispered sadly, "I'm so sorry Zora. You really are here aren't you? It's just that you were gone for eight years, and so everyone assumed you weren't ever coming back. Your parents even held a funeral for you. Lots of people were there."

I felt tears begin to prick the corners of my eyes when he said this last part and I choked out, "A ... a funeral? But I'm not ... I'm not dead."

Denver laughed uneasily and replied, "Well yeah ... I see that now. And hey ... to make you feel better, your parents waited a few months before they finally were sure you weren't coming back. Even though Lucky had made it quite clear that you were never coming back, your parents and your brother were the last to give up hope."

I muttered, "But they did give up hope in the end."

Lucky interjected here, "Zora. I *told* them you weren't ever coming back so that they might understand. I was surprised they waited as long as they did."

I was still a little upset, but I understood what Lucky was getting at. Denver suddenly asked, "How long are you staying, Zora? Do you have to go back, or are you here to stay for good?"

"Well I can be here until the sun comes up, and then I have to go back, but I'm allowed to visit again. I'm not sure when it will be though, because the times between the Land of Inspiration and Earth are so different. Time doesn't seem to pass as quickly there, and quite frankly, I can't tell if time passes at all. I'm immortal now, that's why I have to go back."

Denver questioned, "Immortal?"

I noticed he now regarded me with a strange expression as if I was some bizarre creature. My cheeks suddenly grew hot and I cried out, "I did not choose to be who I am! Denver, please don't look at me like that—I've always admired you. I've just never had the courage to talk to you because that stupid Serpent was trying to destroy me and Lucky had warned me of him, and—," I groaned in frustration but muttered, "You know what? Maybe it wasn't the Serpent that was ruining me. Maybe it was just the fact that you seemed so perfect, and I couldn't have one conversation with you that I didn't regret later. The things that

I said to you … I always wondered why I even said them in the first place!"

Lucky cut in, "But Zora! The Serpent even told you he had been torturing you ever since he knew you had the Golden Happiness."

"No Lucky," I retorted, "You said the Serpent feeds off negative thoughts right? Maybe by me being infatuated with Denver gave the Serpent some sort of advantage over me, but the conversations he had nothing to do with. I realize that now. The Serpent was the voice inside my head telling me that I would never be loved because all of my conversations I messed up. He even told me I wasn't pretty enough— that I would live life alone and unloved. I shouldn't have listened, because you were telling me otherwise and you're my guardian, not the serpent, but I did listen to him, and I kind of closed myself into a … a blanket of silence. I felt I was under some sort of curse that I longed to break free of, but I never could."

Lucky looked at me, mouth agape, and Denver was equally shocked. Lucky was finally able to stammer, "But … but the Dove of Light … you have the Golden Happiness … what you say cannot be true."

"Lucky," I objected, "I know you are trying to protect me from the truth, but I have to face it. I wasn't strong enough at first to fight the shadowy creatures—I let them take over—and it wasn't until the Serpent finally broke into this world and threatened to kill Denver that I finally found my voice. The Golden Happiness has to deal with some sort of love. Perhaps that is why it needed to be in this world in order to grow."

There was a long silence, which Lucky broke, murmuring in awe, "Of course … you're right, Zora."

I looked at Denver and then sighed in despair when I realized this was yet another conversation that I wished I had rather not had, but Denver only asked, "So you're immortal?"

The question brought me back to what he had said about my parents and my funeral and I buried my face in my hands and tried to hide the tears that ran down my cheeks. My voice shook when I answered quietly, "Yes … but I don't want to be. I want to be here … I want to be with my friends and family, but I … I can't if I'm immortal."

"Why not?"

Denver's question frustrated me. Two simple words and I suddenly lost it. The tears streamed down my face steadily, and I sobbed, "Because if I'm immortal then all of my loved ones would die before me, and I would be left to roam this Earth alone. Please, try to understand. I know this is all very strange, but I'm still me ... I'm still Zora!"

Lucky filled in what I left out, "Her immortality is like a curse in a fairy tale and she needs 'Prince Charming' to break it."

I couldn't stop the tears from coming, though I tried with all my might. What Lucky said was true, but I didn't want Denver to hear it, and I especially didn't want him to see me crying. I wanted so desperately to get away, but I couldn't until the sun came up. I began to loathe myself in a way I could not explain. And then the unexpected happened—I felt Denver pull me towards him and he held my head against his muscular chest, trying to soothe me. He wrapped his other arm around my back and patted me comfortingly as he murmured, "I didn't mean to upset you, Zora. I'm just really confused. Please don't cry."

He rubbed his hand through my hair, and when my sobbing finally ceased, I pulled gently away and sighed glumly, "I'm fine ... I'm okay ... it's just stressful not remembering exactly who I am." I paused and then whispered, "Thank you ... but why would you comfort me? I always thought that you thought I was annoying."

He kissed my forehead gently and my heart burned with passion at the touch, and I was relieved when he replied, "For the hundredth time, I'm not annoyed with you for acting like a high school girl. Here, maybe this will help you."

Before I could ask what he meant, he took off my crown and placed it on the end table, and when he turned back to me he continued, "There. Do you feel better? You're not a queen. You're just Zora ... like you said you wanted to be."

The crown had never really bothered me, but for some reason, I suddenly felt as if a great burden had been lifted. I nodded and then asked, "Can you tell me what happened that last day? Like second by second? I need to know everything."

Denver hesitated, "Everything? Well ... I don't know. I mean, just to sum it up, you saved the world and I almost got killed by this creepy serpent that kept saying he was going to submerge the world in darkness and unhappiness. It's hard to really say what happened. It was so bizarre and it happened all so fast."

Lucky suddenly jumped up on the bed in between us and said, "I can help you with that. I'll tell both of you exactly what happened that day. I can't show you through memories though, Zora, because the sun is gone, but I'll try as best I can not to leave anything out."

I looked at him and questioned, "You'll really tell me now? No leaving anything out?"

Lucky shook his head and he stretched out on the bed and put his paws on my lap and then began, "It was graduation day, as you have heard so many times before. You were walking up to get your diploma, Zora. They had just called your name, and at the same time, I had abruptly felt myself being pulled towards the Land of Inspiration. Conrad was calling me to tell me to bring you there, because almost the whole land had been destroyed and the Serpent was trying to break into this world.

"As soon as Conrad told me you needed to be brought to the Land of Inspiration, I tried rushing back to get you, but for some reason the Serpent had crushed through the portal and beat me there. I couldn't get through the portal and I panicked. The Serpent had left a black cloud in its place and I was so frightened for what would become of you. But the Dove of Light quickly came to my aid, for He had been fighting the Serpent, but when I entered the Land of Inspiration, I had caused enough distraction for the Serpent to slither past.

"The Dove of Light immediately began shining and then He passed some sort of power to me as well and I was glowing too. Then He told me to hurry and get you or the whole world would be destroyed. So I went through that scary black cloud where the portal had been, because I knew I had to rescue you … and the world. But when I dropped from the sky into your world again, I had no idea that every person would be able to see me.

"I felt so many eyes on me and I felt the shock of all the people, but what I was watching was you Zora … and do you know what happened when I came through that portal?"

I shook my head, but somehow I started to remember what Lucky was talking about. Visions flashed through my head.

Lucky continued, "I saw the Serpent lunge towards Denver and fear whelmed up in my heart when I realized what you were going to do. Foolish you … my foolish, little Zora … you jumped in between the Serpent and Denver. The Serpent wanted you to do that, Zora, because he knew if you died in this world then all hope would be lost. The Golden Happiness would've been destroyed. But I reacted quickly and I jumped in front of you at the last minute."

Lucky paused and I was startled to see tears streaming down his cheeks and I asked, "Lucky?! What's the matter?"

Lucky shook his head and murmured, "It's nothing … I was just so scared. The memory is still so fresh in my mind. What you were about to do … you're so crazy. But that's okay … I still love you. You're still my little girl."

Denver interrupted here and said quietly, "Lucky. You got hurt when you jumped in between the Serpent and Zora. I remember … he struck you in the shoulder and you were bleeding."

As soon as Denver said this, the memory became crystal clear to me, and I recalled kneeling at Lucky's side and crying, "Lucky! Oh Lucky—no!" I remembered all the blood and I looked at Lucky now and asked, "How are you alive? I remember that … I remember trying to make the bleeding stop, but there was so much and I … I was helpless."

Lucky licked my cheek and then replied, "I am a guardian and besides, we went to the Land of Inspiration shortly after and I was healed. I can not die if you are still living. Guardians never die … they are just sometimes forgotten. When the Dove of Light gave me some of His power to get through to this land, He had made me so that all humans could see me, and that's why I bled. But let me continue.

"You were trying to comfort me … trying to make the bleeding stop like you said, and that's when I told you we had to leave. I could barely stand your misery … I knew you didn't want to leave—you were hesitating and looking at your friends and family as tears streamed down your face. So I had to say, to persuade you, 'Now Zora, or everything will be destroyed—the good Earth and Heaven alike! Denver and your family and friends—they'll all die if you don't come right now!'

"Zora, I hated using your infatuation for Denver against you, but we were running out of time, and we had to go. The Dove of Light always knows what's best and so I trusted that we would get through whatever he put us up against—and we did get through it. I can see that now, and I hope you can too."

I looked at Lucky and fresh tears began to prick the corners of my eyes, but I would not let them fall this time—I had to be stronger than that. And suddenly, a wave of memories all came back to me, and I remembered at once the day which Lucky spoke of. I whispered huskily, "The Serpent made fun of me for loving; he said it was my weakness ... I remember now—his cruel laugh that caused me to weep angry tears, but I spoke against him and told him how I would use love against him."

Lucky smiled and responded, "And so you have. That's why the Golden Happiness was able to be used against him, because you loved when he could not. The Serpent is full of hatred and that is all he knows. Love will always be stronger than hate, no matter the circumstance."

I nodded and then I looked at Denver and laughed awkwardly, "Wow ... I'm really sorry about all this. I wish Lucky would've told me before we came here. I wish you wouldn't have had to witness this."

Before Denver had a chance to reply I got up and moved away towards the window and looked outside at the fading moon and murmured, almost to myself, "Do you think I could ever be a normal human being again? This isn't how things are supposed to be ..." I trailed off, not sure if I wanted an answer or not.

I heard Denver move behind me and within seconds he was standing behind me and he pulled me into his arms and held me there comfortingly. He stated musingly, "You are a normal human being—you just got caught up in some sort of fantasy land that needed your help. You can stay here and meet your friends and family again. You can start right back up from where you left off. Trust me ... I'll help you."

There was silence while he waited for my reply. Finally I whispered, "There are some things I have to think over first, but I want to believe that what you say is true." I glanced outside again, and I started to feel a tingling sensation in my body ... the sun was about to rise. Lucky sensed it too and he barked once towards the window. I muttered, "I know Lucky ... the sun is coming."

Denver looked at me perplexed and questioned, "What?"

I explained hurriedly, "I'm sorry Denver … I have to go back. I told you that. I can't stay here for good yet, but I'll be back. I promise. I don't know when, but please, if tonight meant anything to you at all, trust me and know that I'll come back."

Lucky and I began to glow a golden yellow and the sun's rays began to peek up over the horizon. Denver stepped away from me, looking both confused and a little frightened, as he asked, "What?! Zora, why … where? I don't understand."

Lucky moved over towards me and he jumped into my arms and as our bodies began to vanish, I cried, "Just trust me, and I'll try to find it in me to trust you! I'll be back, and I'll stay if you promise to wait for me! This was not a dream, but farewell for now!"

There was a quick blinding flash of light and we vanished from Denver's room.

Chapter 8

Zora

I was suddenly standing outside the castle of the Land of Inspiration with Lucky in my arms. I put Lucky down and he looked up at me and said cheerfully, "Well, Zora! It looks as though we did it!"

I looked at him with an arched eyebrow and asked sardonically, "Did what? What exactly did we accomplish? All I managed to do was cry in front of him and apologize over and over. I'm pretty sure he thinks I'm pathetic."

Lucky frowned and replied, "Well I'm not going to disagree with you about the crying, but … he did comfort you. Zora, why do you have to be so blind? Can't you think you ever deserve something wonderful in life? You're the girl of his dreams I'm sure. Why would he have objected to you leaving in the end if you weren't?"

I glared at him now and cried out, "That was *the* most awkward conversation I've had with him in my entire life! And I've had some pretty awkward conversations! I don't see how this is going to solve anything." I paused and look around the castle and then asked, "And where's Silvershoes? I thought he was supposed to meet us when we got back."

Lucky was stunned to silence and a voice behind me answered timidly, "I am here Queen Zora, but why are you so upset? Why do you not trust your guardian?"

I whirled around and saw Silvershoes towering over me and I retorted, "The whole time I was there, I was either stammering or crying. I couldn't explain anything correctly. And I do trust Lucky—he finally told us the story of graduation day, but I just don't trust his judgment in this situation."

Silvershoes turned his great, brown eyes on me and asked, "Well would you trust me then? I am Denver's guardian anyway … I would know what he thinks of you. Lucky always knows what you're thinking."

I huffed and hesitated, but I muttered nonetheless, "Okay. What is he thinking then? Or what was he thinking of me?"

Silvershoes smiled and replied, "Well when he first saw you he thought, 'This must be a dream … or she is an angel.'"

I interjected, "That's a lie."

Silvershoes cleared his throat in irritation and continued, "No … it is no lie. He continued to think it was a dream until Lucky bit him, and then he was mostly convinced that it was not a dream. When he was listening to your story and what your options were, he felt pity for you and he was constantly trying to think of a solution. Then, when Lucky told of graduation day, his old love for you was fully restored. He knows how much you care for him."

I listened to Silvershoes in disbelief, but he was still talking, "And then, when you left, he felt dismayed and wished you would have stayed longer. He wanted to know of the place you were staying. Now, he is pondering whether or not it really was all real, but he sees your crown you left there and is convinced, and I am convincing him through his conscience that it was all real."

I patted the top of my head and grumbled sarcastically, "Oh great— this is all just wonderful. I left my crown there! I hope I don't get in trouble."

Lucky bit my dress and pulled on it sharply. When he let go he scolded, "Zora! Are you listening to Silvershoes? Don't worry about that silly old crown—it was probably through the Dove of Light that you left it there anyway. The crown is proof for Denver that you were there, and now he can not say that it was all a dream."

I sighed, "Okay, okay. Maybe you two are right, but now what do I do?"

Lucky and Silvershoes looked at each other, and it was plainly seen that they did not know the answer to my question. But suddenly there was a shout from afar, "Hey! Queen Zora—what is going on?!"

I recognized the voice instantly—it was Emily. She was trotting over to us from a meadow and a mixture of fear and anger were on her face, as well as confusion. When she reached us she rambled on, "Why are you going back? Why would you leave this wonderful land?"

Before I could explain, I heard wings above me and Conrad landed at my side with the same accusing stare as Emily. He whimpered though, rather than demanded, "Why are you leaving us Queen Zora? I thought you were our friend."

"I am—" I began.

Unexpectedly, I heard many voices coming from all around me as creatures—some exotic, and others more ordinary, rushed over from random places. The deer came from the meadow, more dragons and creatures of flight were swooping in from the sky, and rodent-like creatures hopped over from burrows. Reptiles and amphibians ran out of forests and from ponds, and they all made a circle around me looking for an answer. I heard some shouting:

"Don't leave, Zora!"

"We'll miss you ... please don't go!"

"The shadowy creatures will return!"

"The Serpent will come again!"

And then surprisingly, I heard shouts from different creatures answering:

"Oh you old guardian, you ... the Serpent won't ever return here!"

"Zora deserves to finish her life!"

"Don't you know the good queen is trapped here? This is like a prison to her—let her go so she may be with her friends and family again!"

I looked at Lucky, overwhelmed by all the shouting. Some of these guardians I had never even seen before, but suddenly they were all so worried. Lucky saw my look of exasperation and shouted very loudly, "QUIET!!!!"

The creatures were all hushed instantly, and I wondered how Lucky had managed to shout so loud. Lucky huffed and then shouted out so all could hear him, "Look now here, you creatures that call yourselves guardians, yet need Zora to protect you! We have talked to the great

Dove of Light and we have heard Him say that if Zora returns to Earth, the Serpent will still stay in the Sea of Interference. The Serpent's plan to overwhelm Earth in despair is completely destroyed and it will never be pursued again. So why trap Zora here when it is clear she does not belong? We should not keep her trapped in this land, or she will never go to the Sun of Happiness."

A gray porcupine with a blue feathered tail objected grumpily, "This place is not so bad Lucky. It is the same as the Sun of Happiness in beauty!"

Lucky shook his head and growled, "You do not know that for sure. Why do you not understand, you old foolish guardians? Zora is a human being, not a guardian like us. She has family and friends at home that she misses, but she will never see them if she stays here."

There was silence and then the dinosaur with the jaw disorder that I had seen in Conrad's memories stepped forward and added, "Haven't we meddled in this human's life enough? Had it not been for her, we would all be dead! Let's show her our appreciation by letting her return home. Besides, if Lucky said he has spoken to the great Dove of Light, and He says no harm will come to us or the humans by letting her go, then shouldn't we trust him?"

Some of the creatures hung their heads in shame while others murmured quiet agreements, but Emily was not finished with her doubts. She asked loudly, "But my fellow creatures, is it right to send Zora back when we know she may be suffering her whole life there because it is not as beautiful and carefree as this one?"

The creatures were in silence as they pondered this, but the dinosaur-like creature countered, "Well, Emily. I think all of us guardians could agree that the decision is up to Zora and *her* guardian. Not us. They will know what's best … we have our humans to protect and Lucky has his. The Dove of Light watches us all, and so whatever happens is usually for the best. Have faith dear friend! Stop meddling where you are not wanted."

The creatures began to disperse and the dinosaur watched them go in approval. He ignored Emily's cold stare, for he knew he had made his point quite clear. Emily huffed, turned to me and said quickly and quietly, "My apologies, Queen Zora, but I do ask that you think this well and through before you make your decision."

Then she left with Conrad trailing behind her. The dinosaur creature looked at me with his cunning golden eyes and said, "I am sorry all this drama happened, but don't let it affect your choice. You can't find true love here."

Before I could thank him, he took off running. I watched him disappear into a forest and then I looked down at Lucky and stated, "Well now that that's over, what now?"

The answer came from Silvershoes, "I suppose if it's at all important to you, you could retrieve your diary and write down what happened like you used to."

He said this with amusement and I smiled in spite of myself and said, "Yeah … I suppose I could do that. Where is my diary though?"

Lucky barked and then dashed into the castle. Silvershoes and I followed him quickly. Lucky was at the pink door with the roses painted on it and I opened it up and murmured, "Oh … that's right, but I thought the Dove of Light had it last."

As soon as I had the door opened, Lucky bolted in and ran over to the glass table, nearly knocking it over in the process, and grabbed the diary and the pen that were there. Then he ran back over to me and I took the items from his mouth and then swiftly opened the diary. Lucky's tail wagged in excitement as he watched me write:

I haven't written in a long while … eight years I suppose it's been since I was taken from Earth to the Land of Inspiration so I could save the world from an evil Serpent. I have recently regained my memory and today I was finally allowed back to Earth to see Denver Trievus. He is just as amazing now as he was eight years ago, although he seems more mature. Lucky, my guardian, and Silvershoes, Denver's guardian, say that he likes me, but I don't know.

Lucky frowned when he saw me write the last part, but it was true, I didn't know. Silvershoes exclaimed, "Look! It's the Dove of Light! He must have something important to tell you."

Silvershoes was looking outside the castle, and I saw a great golden ray of light. The light's source was indeed a great white dove. Lucky, Silvershoes, and I made our way out of the castle, and I said in cheerful greeting, "Hello! How are you, great Dove of Light?"

The Dove of Light smiled and responded, "I am well, thank you. And I suppose you are well too? I have important information for you involving your next visit with Denver."

I waited patiently for Him to continue—to ask about the crown—but He only examined me thoughtfully and asked, "What is troubling you, little one?"

It should've come to me with no surprise that He knew what I was thinking, but I still hesitated before I replied, "Well … I don't know if Denver thinks I am real or not. For the most part, he thought everything was a dream. And I cried in front of him, though I didn't mean to."

He put a wing around my shoulder and said softly, "Everything will explain itself in time. Just wait a while … be patient for me. Trust the guardians and me … Denver knows you are real. As for now, you will prepare to visit him again. I am going to ask you to bathe and then go to your room and sleep. When you wake up again, you will bathe once more, and then the appropriate attire for your next visit will be given to you. Go now, little one, and do not fret about what occurred between you and Denver on your visit. It was all very fine actually."

Before I could speak, He spread out His magnificent wings and flew back up towards the bright Sun of Happiness, and I was left standing there with Lucky and Silvershoes. Lucky was quiet, but Silvershoes was anxious and pushed me towards the castle doors and insisted, "Go on Zora—take your bath and then take your nap, for time passes while you dawdle, and Denver awaits for your return. Hurry … please."

The urgency in his voice, made me hurry inside the castle and up the stairs to the bathroom. I closed the door and then quickly stripped the dress and undergarments off and stepped into the already filled tub. The bubbles smelled of lavender and by no doubt were there to soothe me and help me to sleep better afterwards. I tried to relax, because I knew that's what the Dove of Light had meant the baths to be—comforting—but I was only able to stay soaking in the waters for about fifteen minutes before I got restless.

When I stepped out of the tub, a towel appeared in the air as before, and I dried off. Undergarments and a dark blue, silk nightgown were on the sink for me to get changed into. As soon as I had my new clothes on and brushed my hair, I left the bathroom with much haste and went to my bedroom. I passed Lucky on the way, who was sitting at the bottom of the stairs, but he quickly got up and followed me to my bed.

I climbed into the big comfy bed and Lucky lay down at my feet. He didn't fall asleep right away though as he had the previous time, but rather he watched me with gentle eyes and with a soft smile on his face. I gazed back at him sleepily from my pillow and murmured, "What is it Lucky? Why aren't you sleeping, and why are you smiling?"

Lucky replied softly, "Why shouldn't I be smiling? The pain is going away—the pain from your broken heart, and Denver is such a nice boy." Lucky frowned a bit and then continued with a hint of sadness, "I suppose we should have to call him a man now though, eh? But he still has a boyish heart, and a boyish face. It is only his age that makes him a man."

I smiled at Lucky's humor and then I persisted, "But why aren't you sleeping then?"

Lucky shook his head and answered, "I am your guardian, and I am not tired." He rested his head on his paws and pretended a yawn and then added, "But I suppose if me sleeping will make you sleep more easily, then I will. Good night Zora … soon you will return home and you will not be stuck in this waiting room babysitting guardians. Sleep well."

I closed my eyes then and within minutes, I was fast asleep, dreaming of seeing Denver again.

When I woke up, Lucky was still at the edge of my bed, awake and alert. When he saw me sit up, he smiled and asked, "Well young Zora, how did you sleep?"

I stretched my arms and replied dreamily with a smile, "Quite well, thank you. Lucky … I dreamt while I slept. I don't ever remember dreaming here before. It was a strange feeling—but a good sort of strange."

Lucky jumped down from my bed and I got out as well as he exclaimed, "Dreams?! Ah—what wonderful things they are, but I want your life to be just as wonderful. So now you must take another bath as the Dove of Light instructed and then meet me and Silvershoes at the blue door with the yellow stars."

I followed Lucky out of the room and as he joined Silvershoes at the blue door with the yellow stars, I headed up the stairs to the bathroom. I took a bath like the night before, but this time the water smelled of roses. When I dried off, I found that the clothes laid out for me were not as royal looking as I had been used to wearing. Instead, there was a pair of black sweat pants with a white stripe down the sides and a green form-fitting t-shirt. I only hesitated slightly before putting them on. I had to trust that the Dove of Light knew what He was doing.

I ran a brush through my hair, which had dried surprisingly and unrealistically fast, and then I hurried down the stairs to join Lucky and Silvershoes. Silvershoes immediately opened the door with his teeth and when he stood back, he said quickly, "Okay Zora … the door is open and you can go now … the sooner the better."

Lucky looked at my new attire with a hint of amusement and he shook his head and murmured, "I won't question Him, but I wonder what He has planned."

I blushed a little bit, suddenly realizing how different I must look to them, but then I recovered and asked, "Silvershoes—are you able to come with us? Wouldn't you want Denver to see you again?"

Silvershoes shook his head and laughed, "No Zora. Denver is not like you … he has forgotten me and I must stay forgotten until he dies. I am not like Lucky either … even if I were to come with you; I would be invisible to Denver. I lack the power you two share, and besides, I might just be a distraction. My only duty is to be his conscience, guiding him away from wrong."

I nodded my understanding and then Lucky began walking through the door, saying as he went, "Come Zora. Let us not waste anymore time."

I walked through the dark door with Lucky, until the shimmering light engulfed us both. Then we were once more standing in Denver's yard, underneath the moonlight.

Chapter 9

Zora

There was a light on the front door that was lit up, and I looked down at Lucky in joy. We wouldn't have to find the spare key again. We would only have to knock.

We walked up to the front door and I knocked, but Lucky was quick to spot the doorbell and he pushed it with his nose. I heard it ring from inside and I held my breath, feeling anxious. Lucky looked at me with some amusement and questioned, "You aren't nervous are you?" He laughed, though not unkindly, and said, "You do entertain me little one."

I heard a dog barking from inside—Otto—and then the door opened revealing Denver. He looked at me in bewilderment and said, "Zora! I was starting to wonder if you would come back. Then this means I wasn't dreaming … is this another night time visit sort of thing?"

I nodded and hesitated before asking, "How long have I been away? I swear it only felt like a couple of minutes in the Land of Inspiration, but …"

I trailed off, and he answered, "It's been about three weeks, but never mind that, come on in!"

I'm startled, but I managed to smile and I stepped inside his house. He closed the door behind me and Lucky, and Otto immediately jumped up on me, barking excitedly. I gently pushed him off me and bent down to pet him as I laughed, "Aww, hi Otto, did you miss me?"

I stood up again as Denver pointed out, "Otto isn't like Lucky, Zora. He's not going to talk back … but I missed you."

I rolled my eyes but I smiled when I questioned, "Oh did you? Well I'm sorry I kept you waiting then, but I did tell you the times were different. How have you been though?"

"I'm fine, but …" He hesitated. "Are you going to keep coming and going like this? Because it's really hard for me to believe that this is real. How do I know this isn't a dream?"

I was about to protest, but Lucky suddenly jumped up and pushed me in the back and before I knew it, I was falling forward, caught by surprise. I didn't hit the floor, however, because Denver quickly leaned out and caught me. I looked up at him, my face turning red in embarrassment, but he just smiled, and helped me back up on my feet. Then he said, "All right, I'll admit it, this isn't some wonderful dream. This is real. You left your crown here, and that's proof. But do you seriously *have* to come here at night?"

I muttered, "Yes. I'm sorry, I know my visits are causing you to lose sleep, but I have no other choice until my immortality is taken away. Don't ask why … I'm not too sure myself."

Denver shrugged and said, "Actually both of your visits have been on nights where I don't have work the next day, so I sleep after you leave."

This is something the Dove of Light must've planned, I thought to myself. I suddenly caught sight of Denver's red shoes on the floor and said, "You know, I tripped on those shoes on the way in last time."

Denver looked at me and replied with a hint of amusement, "I'm sorry, but normally people don't break into my house in the middle of the night. Though had I known you were coming, I might've put them somewhere out of the way."

I shook my head and laughed, "No. I wasn't criticizing you for leaving your shoes out; I was just remembering how I first admired you for your speed in cross country and track. You know, I was always afraid to admit to people that I actually loved running until I saw that you had a passion for it as well."

Denver raised an eyebrow and questioned, "Oh really?" I nodded and he continued, "Well thank you then."

There was a moment of silence where I abruptly understood the meaning of the clothes I was in. I asked with a smile, "So … do you want to go running?"

I could tell I took him by surprise by the way he abruptly inquired, "Right now … with you? Zora, do you know what time it is? Normally people don't go running at eleven o'clock at night."

I shrugged and answered, "Well I'm not exactly what most people would consider to be a normal person, now am I? Besides, we can stay on the sidewalk, and the moon is really bright tonight." He was still hesitating so I persisted, "I can keep up with you if that's what you're worried about. I'm immortal, and that gives me more speed. You'll be surprised."

He grinned then and finally gave in, "All right. Looks like we're going on a midnight run." He glanced at my bare feet and continued, "But you're going to need shoes … and socks. It's a good thing I have extra of both. Wait right here."

I obliged and he walked out of the hallway and disappeared into another room. While I waited, I bent down to pet Otto again, who was being surprisingly quiet. Lucky, who's next to me, licked my arm and whispered, "Zora, your heart is repairing itself quite nicely, but I fear Gooba's words now. I feel … thinner … like I'm wasting away."

Before I could ask what he was talking about, Denver was back, holding a pair of blue and gray shoes and some white socks. He placed the shoes down and then tossed me the socks. I pulled the socks on as he put on the pair of red shoes. Then, as I was putting on the other shoes, he said, "Zora, I meant to ask you before, but what exactly do you mean when you say you're immortal until you make your decision? I know you probably told me the last time you were here, but could you explain it again? It's really confusing."

I was sitting down, tying the shoelaces when I answered, "Tell me about it. I'm still confused by the whole situation. To make things short, if I decide to stay here, my immortality gets taken away. I have no problem with that, but some creatures in the Land of Inspiration told me that life on Earth is more difficult than living in the Land of Inspiration. So … that's the decision I have to make—an easy life, or seeing my friends and family again. If I stay there, even after my friends and family die, I still wouldn't be able to see them, because they would go up to a different place called the Sun of Happiness."

I stood up and I saw he was looking at me, and after a moment of silence, he stated, "I didn't understand half of what you just said, but isn't it kind of obvious what you should do? You belong here, Zora. With people, not with a bunch of creatures you claim are guardians."

Lucky suddenly jumped towards him, deeply offended, and growled, "The creatures *are* guardians! And they have been the most wonderful friends to Zora! You must try to understand Zora's crisis a little better, Denver. What would you choose if you were in her dilemma? A carefree life where you wouldn't have to worry about work ever again, or where your next meal might come from? Or would you choose to live this mortal life just because there are important people here that you love? Never mind the fact that you'll have to work yourself dead to earn a living."

Denver glared at Lucky and retorted, "So what are you trying to do then? I thought you were Zora's guardian, and that you were supposed to help her make the right choice. Now you're convincing her that Earth is a bad place to be? I don't understand you—I thought you wanted Zora to stay here."

I was irritated that they were talking as if I wasn't in the room, but Lucky only added quietly, "I'm only saying that you have to convince Zora that this place is worth giving up the Land of Inspiration."

There's silence, which I broke, saying, "Come on Denver, let's go for a run."

I opened the door and walked out into the cool night air, inhaling the freshness. Denver's behind me and he closed the door, but not before I saw Lucky lying down on the floor, tears trickling down his cheeks. I wasn't sure what he was crying about, but right then I didn't care. He was making me upset.

Denver trailed over to me and said, "Well, tonight has certainly been dramatic."

I nodded in agreement and sighed heavily, "I'm sorry about Lucky. He's just nervous ... worried that I'll forget him I think. It's so hard to explain ... I wish I was just a normal human being."

He put an arm around my shoulder and said, "You are a normal human being. You've just been through some crazy adventures. Come on ... let's go for a run."

His arm dropped from my shoulder and he jogged down the driveway. I followed and soon we're running next to each other on the sidewalk. We ran until we reached the end of the street. There, Denver slowed down to a stop, and he stared at me with a strange look on his face; we were both breathing a little heavier than usual, but we both knew we could keep going if we wanted to.

When we were both breathing normally again, he said in amazement, "Wow. You really are fast. You just kept up with me for two miles! You could've never done that before."

I grinned and replied, "I know. Isn't it wonderful what immortality can do? I could keep up with you for as long as you wish."

Denver frowned a little and stated, "Hmm ... I'm not so sure I like that. You're not supposed to be as fast as me. So ... if you decide to stay here, you won't be immortal and you'll have to train to maintain your speed like a normal human being?"

I nodded and then pointed out, "Hey ... you said I *was* a normal human being."

"You are ... except for your insane amount of speed and energy all of a sudden."

I looked at him humorously and he shook his head and said, "Never mind. But ... tell me. What would make you decide to stay?"

Denver started walking back down the street again towards his house and I walked by his side. He was watching me, waiting for a response, but I only blushed and looked down and replied, "I'm not really sure ... I ... I have to restore my heart here I think, but ..."

I'm glad it was too dark for him to see me blush, but he didn't let the conversation end. He persisted, "Come on ... you can tell me. What about this restoring your heart? Did the Land of Inspiration make you sick or something?"

"No. It's nothing like that, it's more of a spiritual thing, or ... emotional. I need to ... well ... I'm not sure I should tell you. It's kind of stupid actually, and I don't really want you to ..." I trailed off and looked away from him. How could I tell him that I would stay if I knew he would love me? I couldn't force him into that. It wouldn't be true love then.

My heart skipped a beat when he put his arm around me, and I turned back to look at him again and he said, "Zora, come on. I want you to stay here ... you belong here."

"Well ..." I hesitated, but he didn't move away from me, so I continued, "You know I kind of had this sort of a big crush on you in high school, but I … I thought you were so perfect that I couldn't ever talk to you."

Denver laughed, "I'm not perfect, Zora. Nobody is. And you did talk to me, but it was on the internet." He paused and then added, "That got annoying real fast."

I blushed again and murmured, "I know … I'm sorry. I didn't mean to, really."

He surprised me by merely saying, "That's okay. I forgive you. I kind of missed it when you left. Of course maybe that was because I knew you weren't ever coming back, and that you were forced to leave because you wanted to protect me. But it doesn't matter now—you're back—and now it's my turn to help you."

I heard honesty in his voice and it pleased me, but confused me at the same time. I murmured, "You know … I *still* have a big crush on you."

"I know … that's the reason why you came back, isn't it?"

I nodded, surprised, and said, "But I'm scared to stay. I'm afraid I won't adjust, but I don't want to never be able to see my parents again, or my friends … or … or you."

Denver stopped suddenly and stepped in front of me and then turned so he was facing me. I stared deep into his eyes, unable to look away. His hands were on my shoulders and he leaned towards me and whispered, "Please stay Zora. Try to see you belong here."

Before I could reply, he pulled me closer to him, and before I knew it, I was in a breathtaking kiss. It was slow and loving and completely unexpected. My heart was pounding in my chest and my head was swimming by the time we pulled away from each other.

We're both breathless, as if we had just gone for another mile run, and I was in complete shock. I was numb and couldn't speak, but I was brought back down to earth when Denver apologized, "I'm sorry Zora, I should've—"

I found my voice then, and stammered, "No, no. It's fine. You just … caught me by surprise."

I smiled at him and he returned the smile and said, "Stay with me Zora. This is your home … this is where you belong."

We started walking down the sidewalk again, but before I could say anything regarding Denver's request, I heard three quick barks and recognized them as Lucky's. I saw him seconds later, running down the sidewalk towards us. When he was a few feet away from us, he lunged forward at Denver and growled, "Will you love her if she stays then?! Tell me you will love her … I do not mean to force the matter so, but I am fading."

He sounded fierce when he first approached us, and I was angry with him for being so difficult, but towards the end of his threat I felt and heard the fear and anxiety in his voice. Still, I could not help myself from pushing him away from Denver and crying out, "Lucky! What on earth is wrong with you?! And why are you here—how did you get out of the house?"

Lucky looked up at me, tears streaming down his cheeks, as he choked out, "I only want what's best for you, but I can't stay here very much longer and monitor every step of your life, so I need to make sure there is someone here to take care of you. Zora … look at me … I am fading!"

"I *am* looking at you, Lucky, and you look fine to me."

He shook his head and wept, "Pet me then, if you think I am fine. You're growing up Zora. I can no longer stay here like this."

I reached out to pet him—to prove to him that he was wrong and I was right—but I was dismayed to see my fingers slip through his fur, as if he were just some illusion. I couldn't comprehend what was going on, and I looked at him in question and stammered, "But … but you were never like this before!"

Lucky sighed, and he stopped crying long enough to explain softly, "But I was, Zora. No one ever saw me like this until graduation. I was always invisible to everyone but you. You had always imagined what my fur would feel like, but I am only a guardian … a conscience."

"But the other guardians—" I started to protest.

He shushed me, "In the Land of Inspiration the guardians lose their invisibility and come to life to be seen by all. Everyone who visits the land and the great Sun of Happiness can see them—and not just their own creations, but other peoples' too. You got the opportunity to see that glory early, but now it is time for you to finish your life."

"So …" Denver started to say. It startled me for a moment that he was still there, and then I comprehended what Lucky was saying—what Gooba meant when he was talking about me forgetting him. I could not be with Denver and also keep Lucky visible as a real dog. I had to let one of them go.

"This isn't fair," I complained.

Lucky looked at me with pity and replied softly, "I know ... but everything is going to be okay soon. You'll see ... just trust me."

I glanced at Denver and Lucky followed my gaze and said apologetically, "I'm sorry Denver ... I never really meant to lose my temper. You just have to understand the connection between guardians and their humans. Your guardian would've done the same in my position."

Before Denver could reply, Lucky started walking back down the sidewalk and called over his shoulder, "Come along you two ... we have important people to visit tonight. As I will not be here much longer, we must make this visit as soon as possible. I have some issues to clear up before I vanish."

Denver looked at me perplexed and I shrugged and stated, "Lucky certainly has his mood swings. He hasn't been himself lately."

Without another word, we walked after Lucky back up the sidewalk to Denver's house. As we're heading towards the door to his house, Lucky asked, "Denver—you don't mind driving us someplace tonight, do you?"

I could still tell Denver was just as confused as I was when he replied, "No, but ... where are we going?"

Denver opened the door to the house and the three of us walked into the entrance way as Lucky replied, "Oh, I'll tell you when we're there. Just follow my directions and we'll get there without any trouble. I presume you'll need to get your keys?"

Denver nodded, but turned towards me and asked, "Do you want your crown back first? I'll go get it for you—it's still upstairs."

I replied, "Sure ... it belongs in the Land of Inspiration anyway. I should probably take it back." I grinned and added, "And I *am* queen. I should be wearing it right now."

Denver laughed, "Yeah right. Queen of a fairytale land maybe, but you're not queen here. You didn't even make homecoming queen. Maybe I shouldn't give it back."

I knew he was just teasing, but I slowly started to walk past him towards the darkened rooms and I said, pretending to be hurt, "Ouch. That's cold. I guess I'll just have to get it myself, and then maybe I'll stay in the Land of Inspiration where they know I'm queen."

I turned away from him so he couldn't see me smiling and I darted into the other room and ran to where I knew the stairs were. He yelled after me in concern, "Come on Zora! You know I was just kidding—I want you to stay!"

I heard his footsteps behind me as I ran up the stairs and into his room. It was dark, but the light of the moon outside and the light from the alarm clock guided me to the end table where I saw the crown. I grabbed it and then turned around to see Denver standing in the doorway watching my expression.

I put the crown on my head and stuck my tongue out at him and then exclaimed, "Aha! Now I am queen again! What are you going to do about that?"

Denver grinned and stepped through the doorway and slowly made his way over to me. As he walked, he said, "Someone's full of herself—and I thought I had offended you. That crown's not so special. Want to know why?"

He was a step away from me, and I leaned slightly back against the bed when I replied, "What? Why isn't it spe—?"

I broke off when his lips tenderly brushed against mine and he pulled me gently towards him. I seemed to stop breathing and my heart was pounding so loud, I was sure he could hear it.

Denver took off my crown and then leaned back just enough to answer, "Your crown is made out of *plastic*. I could easily break it if I wanted to."

I pushed him lightly away and scowled, "You wouldn't dare."

He held the crown in front of me and made as if he was about to break it, but I quickly lunged for the crown and protested, "No! Don't break it! I could get in trouble."

Denver held the crown away from me, but let me snatch it away. He looked at me startled, and said humorously, "Whoa. That's a side of you I've never seen. I didn't think you could be aggressive."

I rolled my eyes and then suddenly remembered Lucky was waiting for us downstairs. I walked past Denver and out of his room, as I murmured, "Come on; let's go. Lucky is waiting."

As he followed me he said, "Zora, please don't hate me for what I said. I wasn't thinking. I'm sorry."

I shook my head and stated amusingly, "Never mind. Let's just forget about it. Besides, I've probably annoyed you enough in the past to the point where I deserved it anyway. It doesn't matter right now. Just help me find Lucky."

We wordlessly made our way through the dark rooms to the lighted hallway where we came in, but Lucky wasn't there. I looked at Denver, feeling anxious, and asked, "Do you see him? Where did he go? He didn't follow us upstairs."

He shrugged, just as Lucky called out, "Zora! Zora, I'm here. Right here in this room. Can't you see me? I'm right in front of the door. Don't forget me now!"

As soon as he spoke I saw a flash of golden light, and he flickered into view in front of the door. His image was wavering, as if he was some sort of illusion, and he looked tired. I rushed over to him and tried stroking his head, but my fingers merely slipped through his fur. I cried out, "Lucky, how do I reverse this?! Come back!"

Lucky shook his head, but he smiled when he tried to comfort me saying, "Shush now little one. Just don't leave me alone here—keep talking to me, and I'll be back to normal. But … but Zora, I need you to understand that I won't be here very much longer. You don't need me here anymore … not like this. It would be better if I were just a conscience. Please understand … I don't want any more tears from you."

I nodded, not trusting my voice at the moment. I understood him quite perfectly, but I wished with all my heart that it wasn't true.

Lucky turned towards Denver and asked, "Do you have your keys?"

Denver reached over to a cabinet hanging on the wall, opened it up, and then pulled out a keychain with four different keys on it. He then looked back at Lucky and asked, "All right, here are the keys, now where are we going?"

I was startled to see Lucky walk right through the door as if he were a ghost, and he called over his shoulder, "Just get in the car and I'll tell you on the way. We must hurry though—I am running out of time."

Denver walked past me and opened the door. He waited until I had walked out as well and then he shut the door and locked it. Then we quietly followed Lucky over to the opened garage, me pondering where Lucky was taking us, and Denver probably thinking the same thing.

In the garage was a gray car, and Lucky was quick to say, "Nice car. Unlock the doors and we can be on our way. The quicker we can get there the sooner we can return."

Denver obliged and I opened the passenger's door and Lucky jumped in to sit in the middle. I got in after him as Denver slid into the driver's seat. He started up the car, backed out of the garage, and then asked, "Okay, now where do I go from here? You said you knew where we have to go."

Lucky nodded and replied, "That I do, okay, just follow my directions and we'll get there without a hitch. Turn right out of here and then …"

Chapter 10

Zora

A half hour later we were turning into a driveway of a large, old farmhouse, and I gasped in shock, "Lucky—this is Mom and Dad's house! We're seeing them?"

Lucky opened his mouth and let his tongue hang out in a dog-like smile and I laughed at his expression. After Denver stopped the car and turned the engine off, he turned towards Lucky and asked, "Okay, so explain to me. Why are we here?"

Lucky clarified, "I need to explain to Zora's parents about what happened at graduation. They need to hear the whole story—from beginning to end ... and they need to hear it tonight because I am running out of time and energy. Come on you two, let's go."

Denver unlocked the doors and we all got out. As Lucky led the way to the back door, he mused, "I wonder how your parents are going to act when they're woken up by a talking dog at 1:00 in the morning."

I asked, "Do you think they ever fixed the doorbell?"

"Probably not."

Before I could ask Lucky his plan on getting in then, he trotted off towards an old shed, and I murmured, "Ah ... the spare key."

Denver was standing next to me and stated, "I wouldn't want to be on his bad side. Can you imagine all of the tricks he could play on people?"

I laughed but disagreed, "No. He wouldn't do anything hurtful or mean—even if I asked him to. He does what's right, and if I ever asked him to play a trick on someone, he'd probably scold me. He's my guardian anyway, and his job is to keep me out of trouble ... he wouldn't get me into it."

Denver shrugged and said, "I don't know ... he *bit* me."

I smiled sympathetically and replied, "Oh yeah ... sorry about that, but he was only trying to help me out. You thought I was an illusion, remember?"

Lucky was coming back to us now, the keys hanging from his mouth, but he looked less smug, almost sad. His expression was troubled.

"What's wrong?" I asked, "Are they the wrong keys?"

Lucky shook his head and dropped the keys in my outstretched hand and then replied, "No ... they're the right keys, it's just ... did you hear a dog bark when we pulled in?

Denver looked at me confused, but I understood exactly what he was saying. I murmured, "Oh ... that silly mutt we had. He always barked when people came in. I wonder when ..."

I trailed off, not wanting to think about it. The poor dog would have been twelve years old now. Lucky was quick to say, "Don't assume anything ... maybe he's just gone deaf. But if he has ... passed away, don't despair. Animals may not have guardians—they rely heavily on instinct and owners if they are pets—but I strongly believe they still go to the Sun of Happiness. Never mind that now though. Let's focus on the task at hand."

I nodded and walked up to the back door and unlocked it. Then I opened the door as quietly as I could and we all stepped into the dark house. The entrance way was how I remembered it—to the right was a flight of stairs leading to the basement where the washer and dryer were; to the left, it opened up to a huge room—the kitchen.

Lucky looked up at me and Denver and whispered, "Wait here, and wait as quietly as you can. I will wake up your parents and explain everything to them. Hopefully they will remember me and they won't think their age has fooled them. I am expecting to get it all sorted out in an hour. In the meantime, make yourselves comfortable, but for goodness sakes, *stay quiet.*"

Then, without another word, he disappeared into the darkness, and I knew he was headed up a flight of stairs. In the dark, I could see Denver looking at me, wondering what to do. I put my finger to my lips and then grabbed his arm and carefully led him to the kitchen table so that we could sit while we waited. I was relieved when we finally made it there without tripping over something or making any loud noises.

We sat in silence for a moment, until I heard a shout of alarm—a surprised scream coming from my mom. Lucky must've calmed her down soon after though, because then there was silence and then quiet murmurings. I couldn't make out any words.

Denver looked at me and whispered, "I don't know if I should be here. What are your parents going to think of me being here with you at 1:00 in the morning?"

I replied softly, "Don't worry about it. Lucky's explaining everything … I hope."

"But what if he doesn't? I don't want your parents to think—"

I cut him off, "But I want you to stay here. Don't leave me alone … I'm sure my parents will understand once Lucky's done talking to them."

"Okay, fine … if you say so."

We're silent then and we waited in the dark quiet of the room for about an hour—perhaps it was longer—until finally I heard footsteps clambering down the stairs. Within seconds, Lucky burst into the kitchen with Mom and Dad at his heels. Mom turned on the lights as she and Dad came into the room. Lucky ran over to me and stopped and sat between me and Denver, a satisfied look was on his face.

Mom and Dad were standing in the doorway between the kitchen and the living room, staring at me in happy disbelief. They were as I remembered, except for with a little more gray in their hair.

Mom inquired uncertainly, her voice almost a whisper, "Zora? Is it really you?"

I held out my arms and smiled, although the tears of emotion threatened to break free, and I replied as calmly as possible, "Well … I'm home."

There was a brief pause, and then I ran towards my parents just as they were stepping towards me, and we embraced each other with hugs and kisses and tears of joy.

I said ecstatically, "Oh, I'm so glad to be home! I'm sorry I woke you up, but—"

Dad interrupted, "No! Don't be sorry—we thought Lucky said you were going to be gone forever! This is a wonderful surprise!"

Mom held me in a tight hug as she added, "We love you Zora. Please tell us you're here to stay. Where have you been anyway?"

I pulled away from her and smiled as I replied, "I've been in a wonderful place called the Land of Inspiration—it's where all the guardians of people live."

Mom suddenly caught sight of Denver and asked, "Is this your guardian then? I always thought it was Lucky, or do you have two?"

I almost burst out laughing at the thought. In a way, I guess Denver was sort of like a guardian to me … he could save me from a lonely immortal life. I explained quickly though, "No. Lucky is my guardian—that's why he was able to take me away on graduation day. But never mind that," I gestured towards Denver and said, "He's Denver Trievus. He was in my grade in school—you remember him don't you?"

I felt the tension rise in the room suddenly as Mom said, "Oh. What's he doing here?"

Before I could reply Dad asked sternly, "Zora, how long have you been here, and how long have you been with him?"

Denver began, "Mr. Cummings, I can assure you that—"

But Lucky suddenly intervened, "Don't worry Dad and Mom. Zora was quite safe when she was with Denver. She has only visited him one other time and that was by order of the creator of guardians. I was always with her and I can assure you that nothing terrible happened and she was in good hands. You can trust me … I never lie and I am your daughter's guardian."

Dad seemed to accept this because his expression softened and he changed the subject, and asked, "Are you really here to stay then?"

I hesitated, not sure how to explain, but Lucky answered, "Yes, but she has to go back to the Land of Inspiration one more time to tell the creator of guardians her decision. Then He will take her immortality away and she'll stay here and continue her life as it was before she left … well … her life will *almost* be as normal as it was before she left. You'll have to forgive Zora if she's trouble at first. She's used to an easy life in the Land of Inspiration … it's not quite like this world. Anything she desires is given at her request."

I looked at Mom and Dad and confessed, "That's why I'm not sure I want to stay here. It will be so different, and I don't want to be a burden to you."

Before either Mom or Dad could reply, Denver protested, "But Zora! You already promised me you would stay. I'll help you adjust if that's your biggest fear. And … and you can stay with me if your parents kick you out because you've become a burden. You'd never become a burden to me."

Dad retorted, "That will be quite unnecessary. Zora, you can stay here as long as you wish. Just please come home."

I started to reassure them that I would probably choose to stay, but Lucky also added, "Zora. You have your memory back now. You can't possibly think that you'd be happy living an eternity in the Land of Inspiration without ever seeing your family and friends again. And even after they die, you still wouldn't see them because they would go directly to the Sun of Happiness after reuniting with their guardian. You however would be trapped forever in the Land of Inspiration. It's a lovely place—don't get me wrong—but you would never be happy and your days would be spent wandering aimlessly around in sorrow. It would be like me living without you, it just isn't possible."

Dad said, "I like Lucky. He seems to know what's best."

I rolled my eyes, but Denver agreed seriously, "He truly is an amazing guardian … all that he's done for Zora. It's a shame she doesn't listen to him more often."

I crossed my arms in defeat and muttered, "Okay, okay, I'm staying. I know Lucky's right, I'm just scared that's all, but I know it's the only way to free myself from being trapped in between two lands. So I am most definitely staying here. Happy now?"

Denver stared me straight in the eyes and smiled, and I melted when he replied simply, "For now."

I turned away from him, my heart hammering in my chest, and looked at Mom and Dad again and said, "I can't stay with you tonight though. I'll be back as soon as I am free from the Land of Inspiration. It will be soon, but the time there is different from the time here, so another couple of weeks or even months could pass before I return, but trust me and know that I am coming back."

I gave Mom and Dad another kiss on the cheek and they told me they loved me and I replied, "I love you too. I'll always love you. Don't tell Bradley I'm coming back yet—I want to surprise him."

Dad asked, "Wait—are you planning on surprising him or scaring him?"

I grinned and looked down at Lucky and asked, "I don't know yet, what do you think Lucky?"

Lucky laughed, "Come now Zora. He's really missed you these past eight years—don't startle him too badly."

I started to head out of the house, and Mom asked, "Wait—where are you going?"

I didn't stop walking, but I answered, "I have to go back. I already told you that. The sooner I can return to the Land of Inspiration, the sooner I can rid myself of my immortality and come home. Don't worry, I'll be fine."

Denver was following me out of the house and Lucky's behind him when Dad called out, "Wait! I don't—"

Lucky stopped and I heard him say, "Don't worry, your daughter speaks the truth—she will be fine. I will not let her fall in harm's way. You saw me protect her from the serpent at graduation. What you can do before she returns though, is perhaps buy her some new notebooks and pencils, so that she may write stories again. I'm sure she has many adventures to tell the world."

Then he followed me and Denver outside. We all got into the car again and Denver pulled out of the driveway as he said, "Zora. You know the sun won't be up for another two hours. You didn't have to leave yet if you wanted to talk to your parents longer. I wouldn't have minded."

I smiled and replied, "I know, but I wanted to spend the last few minutes with you instead of with them. I'll have all the time in the world to talk to them when I come back, but tonight I just want to be with you."

He smiled then and said, "I'm not surprised. I'm glad you've finally agreed to stay here on Earth."

I scratched Lucky behind the ears as I replied, "Me too."

It was quiet then until we arrived back at Denver's house. He parked the car in the garage and we got out of the car and went inside the house. We were greeted by Otto, and I petted him as Denver put the keys away. Then he turned the light on in the next room leading from the entrance way. It was a cozy living room with beige carpeting and off-white painted walls. There was a chair and a couch in front of a big plasma-screened TV.

Otto ran into the room after Denver, and Lucky and I followed him. I saw Denver glance at a clock hanging on the wall and he frowned when he stated, "Its three-thirty already. Last time you left at five o'clock. I wish the sun wouldn't come up so early." Then he gestured towards the couch and said, "Would you like to sit?"

I nodded and sat down as Denver grabbed a remote sitting on a table between the couch and the chair. Before he pressed any buttons, however, Lucky pushed the power button on the TV with his nose and then lay down in front of it. Otto curled up next to him and put his head on Lucky's back.

Denver shrugged and put the remote back down and then he sat next to me as he said amusingly, "Well Lucky sure made himself at home."

Lucky turned his head slightly and said, "Shush. I'm watching the News."

Denver looked at me and I rolled my eyes, but we're both quiet for a while, watching words scroll across the bottom of the screen and listening to the news reporter. I wasn't really paying much attention to what was being said though—it was something about stocks that didn't make much sense to me.

After a while, I mused quietly, "I wish I had talked to you sooner … when we were in school I mean."

Denver put his arm around me and replied, "Yeah, I wish I would've known you liked me that much *before* you were taken away."

Lucky turned to us and grumbled, "Oh would you two quit with your 'could've, would've, should've?' Forget the past—you're together now, and that's all that should matter."

Lucky turned back to the TV, and Denver laughed, "I didn't know he was that interested in the News." He paused and then added, "He is right, but let's pretend for a moment that those eight years haven't passed and we're still in high school and we're both eighteen."

I laughed at the irony and said, "Denver, I *am* still eighteen, but go on."

He smiled and continued, "Imagine we both just got our diplomas and the dark cloud never appeared—"

I interrupted him, "I would've told you I liked you because I know I would've regretted not saying it afterwards. Remember when I asked you to dance with me? I remember like it was yesterday. None of my friends thought I was going to do it—they thought I would change my mind at the last second—but I proved them wrong."

I saw Lucky twitch irritably, but he didn't say anything. He was as curious as I was to see where this conversation was going.

Denver laughed, "Yeah … that was pretty surprising. You were the last person I thought would ask me to dance. Too bad it was at prom and then school ended the following week. We never had any classes together, so I couldn't talk to you about it later. That was an amazing dance."

I rolled my eyes and stated, "Don't kid yourself—I was a horrible dancer … I couldn't relax. You were making me nervous."

He shrugged and said, "Whatever you want to believe, but it honestly wasn't that bad. You look cute when you're awkward."

"Thanks," I said sarcastically, but then I pulled away from him and I shook my head as I murmured, "Someone pinch me."

"What?"

"I can't believe what's happening right now … this must be a dream. The guardians must've tricked me somehow. This is too good to be true." Out of the corner of my eye, I noticed Lucky flinched as if someone had just pulled a thorn out of his paw, but he didn't say anything or move, and so I continued, "There's no way … it just seems impossible that you would say these things after only seeing me for two days after eight years have passed. *How* is this possible?"

Denver pulled me into a hug and kissed my forehead and then he replied, "But this is real. You spent an hour trying to convince me the same thing the moment you came back. I finally believed you and now you're questioning *me?*"

I hesitated, but then I asked quietly, "But how is it you came to like me so quickly? I'm nothing special, I'm only—"

He cut me off, "Zora, you saved my *life* and in doing so you showed the whole school how much you cared about me. That meant a lot to me … and when you were gone …" he paused, as if not certain that he should continue, but then he rushed on, "I tried to forget about you because we were told you were never coming back. But relationships never really worked out for me because I always found myself wondering about you."

I looked at him, disbelieving, and he groaned, "Ugh—you're so difficult, Zora. I don't understand you sometimes, but that's also one of the reasons why I like you … you can be so mysterious. You're here because of me though—ask Lucky. He's your guardian … he knows. We're meant to be together."

Those last words startled me, and I felt Lucky start to relax—he knew Denver was right. And so did I. I said quietly, "Of course … I'm sorry. I … I know this is real, it's just hard to believe."

I rested my head on his shoulder and he held me close to him and he whispered, "I wish you didn't have to go back in the morning. You always claim you're only gone for a little while, but I have to wait three weeks or maybe longer this time, before you come back. I'm afraid you'll change your mind if I'm not there to convince you otherwise. You said so yourself that the place is like Heaven."

"Mmm," I agreed, "But there are no people there, only guardians. I get lonely. You have to trust me … I'm coming back and staying … for good."

To reassure him, I kissed him quickly on the lips, and then I pulled away, blushing, but he only pulled me back towards him and murmured, "Let me be your Prince Charming."

How could I refuse his request? His lips were on mine, crushing the breath out of me in a passionate kiss. I wished I could've stayed longer there in his arms, but suddenly I felt the tingling sensation in my body and Lucky and I began to glow brightly. How had an hour and a half passed so quickly?

I pulled away from Denver and cried out in alarm, "I'm sorry! I'm forced to leave, but I wish I could stay longer … I'll come back as soon as possible, I promise!"

Lucky jumped into my arms and I stood up and backed away from the couch, but with a deep feeling of regret. Denver reached out for me and said, "Wait—please don't go!"

I shook my head and my eyes started to tear up. I couldn't explain to him any clearer why I had to leave—he'd just have to trust me. Lucky and I vanished in a shower of golden light and we were standing once again in the Land of Inspiration. My heart was aching for Denver though, and I hardly noticed the land's extraordinary beauty. What was this beauty compared to my love for Denver?

I set Lucky down. We were outside the lonely castle. Lucky looked up at me and he barked joyously, "Zora, the Dove of Light is coming to send you home ... I can feel Him!"

But before the Dove of Light came, I saw Silvershoes walking towards me, looking the happiest I had ever seen him. When he was standing directly in front of me, he said, "Well done, Zora. You see I speak the truth now? He cares about you ... he does love you."

I laughed shakily, "Yeah ... by some crazy miracle ... or maybe you somehow convinced him that I was his true love."

Silvershoes shook his head and answered, "No. The Dove of Light probably consulted with Gooba a long time ago to make sure that you two would eventually find each other again ... even if it did take eight years. The only thing I did was remind Denver how much he had admired you in high school. You are a good person, Zora. Never let anyone tell you different."

I hugged Silvershoes and whispered, "Thank you. You've helped me heal."

Then I looked down at Lucky and I threw my arms around him and murmured, "And thank you. You're the best friend I could ever ask for. Without you, I wouldn't have seen Denver again ... or any of my other friends and family. You never gave up on me until I remembered. I'm sorry I brought so much pain upon you."

Lucky licked my tearstained cheek and replied gently, "No Zora ... it is not your fault you were chosen as the keeper of the Golden Happiness, or that the guardians erased your memory. I was glad to help you, my friend. And besides, I am your guardian, little one. How could I not help you when I felt your pain?"

I withdrew from him and repeated, "Thank you. You're the best."

Then I stood up and finally looked around at the beauty of the Land of Inspiration—taking it all in. It was true that there was no place on Earth that was as beautiful as this, but I knew I would terribly miss Denver and my family and friends if I stayed. I inhaled the sweet scent of the air and smiled sadly and sighed, "I'm going to no doubt miss the peace of this land."

Lucky looked around as well and said softly, "Ah ... this place is lovely, but you wouldn't be happy here. You would be lonely. I am a guardian and a friend, but I am not human, and I certainly can't replace the part of your heart where Denver is."

I rubbed his head and he smiled his dog smile with his tongue hanging out of his mouth. There was a sudden bright light shining down on me, and I looked up to see the Dove of Light descending towards the ground next to me.

When He landed, He looked upon me with those gentle eyes and asked, "Well? Are you ready to go home now? You have been through much, little one, but I am happy to say you can return now."

I returned His smile and said, "I'll be glad to return, but I'm a little scared."

The Dove of Light shook His head and responded, "Don't be. You will be fine—Gooba has assured me this. I will not tell you your future, however, but it is a good life you will have. Now ... I will take the Golden Happiness and immortality away and set it free in this land, but that does not mean I take away *your* happiness. You understand this, yes?"

I nodded and asked, "The Golden Happiness had to do with love, didn't it? The power only grew because I used love against the Serpent, right?"

The Dove of Light's smile widened, and He replied, "Ah yes. Now you finally understand ... of course, you knew that all along. Now, there will be no pain when I take the immortality and Golden Happiness away. Tell me when you're ready."

I looked around me one last time, observing the beautiful land around me that I wouldn't see again until I was dead. I saw the flowers and the trees, and I heard the rush of water and the chirping of birds. I watched the many different kinds of creatures frolicking happily in the land—some of them were really bizarre and others were more natural, but they were all unique and they were all guardians.

I turned back to the Dove of Light and breathed, "I'm—"

"Wait!" The muffled voice came out of nowhere and I turned to see Emily running at me from inside the castle. In her mouth was a golden apple, and when she stopped in front of me, she looked at me with mournful eyes and nodded towards my hand. I held out my hand and she dropped the apple in it as she huffed, "I'm sorry for everything, Zora. Please forgive me. I turned a blind eye towards Denver and didn't see his love for you, and so I prolonged your healing. I'm so sorry."

I looked at the apple and I saw the words, "The best beauty is not in outer appearances, but rather it is found in the hearts of those who are not afraid to love."

I glanced back at Emily and asked, "What's this for?"

Emily quickly glanced at the Dove of Light before replying hastily, "Just in case Denver ever stops loving you, but I doubt he ever will. The Dove of Light wouldn't tell me what Gooba said your life would be like when you went back home, and so I asked Him a favor, and He allowed me to give you this gift. This amulet will call Lucky back to you if you ever forget him and you really want him back. Through Lucky and the apple, you then can come back, but please don't use this unless absolutely necessary. I hope you'll never have to use it."

I looked at the golden apple in awe and murmured, "Thank you … but why would you give this to me?"

Emily looked away from me and I saw tears slip down her cheeks as she answered, "Because I could feel your pain, and the only thing keeping me from telling you how to find your way back was my own fear … fear that the shadows would return … and fear that Denver wouldn't care if you went back. I see now that I'm wrong. This gift is so that you may forgive me."

I couldn't help but feel angry towards her, but I calmed myself and was thankful of her thoughtful gift. A sudden thought tugged at my mind and I asked, "How can you feel my pain? Whose guardian are you?"

Emily didn't give me a direct answer. Rather she stated, "Think of all of the people you told of Denver Trievus. Then think of each of their reactions. She told you to be careful because she didn't want you hurt if he was just being nice to you at the dance. Sometimes you have to be careful and not get your hopes up too high, or you end up feeling miserable in the end if they're crushed."

I thought about her words and then I thought of all my relatives and friends. Just when I was about to clarify whose guardian she was, she murmured, "I'm your mother's guardian. She was always worried about your obsession with him. And when you were taken away, I knew she wanted you back, but she also kept telling herself that you were in a better place, and I knew you were. Or … at least I thought you were. Here, there were no boys for you to have to worry about, but when I erased your memory of Denver, I saw my mistake when I felt your heart breaking and turning dark. I didn't mean to, Zora. I was just trying to protect you, but all I did was prolong your happiness."

Emily was so choked up on herself, that I just had to give her a quick hug and try to comfort her by saying, "Everything's going to be okay now, Emily. Please don't cry. I've honestly had enough tears."

Emily nodded and tried to smile. The Dove of Light spoke again, "Now Zora, I will teleport you back to Denver's house. It will be Friday afternoon in August when you get there. And Denver will have work off until the following Monday."

I exclaimed, "So you were behind these well-planned nights!"

He smiled and replied, "I didn't want Denver to use the excuse that he had to stop talking to you because he had to go to sleep so he could get up for work the following day."

I shook my head and smiled in amusement. Then the Dove of Light continued, more quietly now, "Zora, you do understand that Lucky will *always* be with you, even though you may not be able to see him, correct?" I nodded and he continued, "Good, now I will take the immortality and Golden Happiness away. Ready?"

I nodded again and He embraced me in His wings and I began to glow brightly. There was a whooshing noise and a yellow orb shot out from my chest. The Dove of Light let me go, and I watched in awe as the orb changed to cherry-red and took the form of a heart. Then it exploded and pieces of the heart scattered about the Land of Inspiration, giving it an even more glorious appearance. I didn't have much time to admire it though, because the Dove of Light took me in His wings again and squeezed me tight as He said gently, "I love you O Chosen One—now go and live your life!"

Chapter 11

Zora

There was a blinding flash of light, and I closed my eyes. I felt the Dove of Light let me go and when I opened my eyes, I was standing in Denver's yard once again. Only this time, the sun was shining brightly in the blue sky. I noticed I was wearing blue jeans, a green blouse, and a pair of pink and silver tennis shoes—a gift from the Dove of Light by no doubt.

I looked over at the driveway and saw him coming out of the garage. When he saw me, he looked startled and he questioned, "Zora? Ohmygosh—you came back! It's been almost a month, and I was—"

I interrupted him, "Hey now, I told you the time passed differently there. It felt only like ten minutes. Besides, I promised I would come back … you've got to have a little more faith in me."

I walked towards him as he walked towards me and he said, "I know, I'm sorry. I guess I'm just more surprised that you came back during the day." He paused and then asked, "Where's Lucky?"

I swallowed hard, and replied in a low voice, "I don't think he was able to come back with me. I wish I would've been able to spend one last day with him though."

Denver started to say sorry, but suddenly much to my surprise, I heard Lucky shouting, "Zora! I am still here, but this is my last day here in this form. Turn and look, I've been here all along. I'll always be here."

I turned and saw him trotting up the driveway, his tongue hanging out in his dog-like smile. He stopped a few feet in front of me and sat. Then he looked at Denver and said seriously, "I brought her safely back, now it's your turn to guide her through the rest of her life and re-teach her the ways of this earth. My time like this is fading—talking dogs don't really exist here—only in one's imagination."

Denver nodded, but I said, "Aw Lucky, why do you always have to be so downhearted? If you really think this is your last day, then you should enjoy it. Stop worrying about me, I'll be fine."

Lucky's grin widened and he replied, "Fine, but only because you asked so nicely."

Then before I could say anything else, Lucky ran into the garage and when he came back out, he was holding a basketball in his mouth. How he had managed to open his mouth that wide was beyond me, but it was quite a sight to see.

Lucky put the basketball down between his front paws and then bowed down in a playful manner, his bottom sticking up in the air and his tail wagging. Then he barked, "Catch me if you can!"

Without another word, he grabbed the basketball in his mouth again and ran towards the backyard. Denver and I exchanged a quick glance before Denver started running after Lucky, yelling, "Hey, you better not chew a hole in that!"

I laughed and ran to catch up with him. The backyard had freshly mowed grass and it was empty save but a few trees and shrubs. Lucky was on the opposite side of the yard, staring at Denver with mischievous eyes. Denver ran over to Lucky, but Lucky didn't move until Denver lunged toward him. At that moment, Lucky jumped over his head and ran towards me, but before he could get any closer, I jumped towards him and tackled him to the ground, wrestling the basketball out of his grip.

Lucky let go of the basketball, and chuckled, "Looks like you still have your speed, but don't forget that you'll have to run just about every day to keep in shape."

"What are you, my coach?" I asked.

Lucky shook his head and answered, "Nope; just a friend that doesn't want to see you sad."

Denver walked over to us and sat down next to me. He looked at the basketball in disgust and complained, "Ugh … dog drool."

Lucky looked at him with apologetic eyes, but then barked and licked his face. Denver pushed Lucky away and then wiped his face as he muttered, "I forgot he could understand me and likes to play jokes."

I laughed and Denver smiled. Then I heard Otto barking from inside the house, and Denver said, "Wait here a minute, I'm going to go let Otto out."

I nodded and he stood up, but he hesitated and looked at me uncertainly. Finally I said, "I'm not going to disappear again. I'm here to stay—I promise."

He seemed to accept this, for he continued on his way to the house. After a few minutes of silence, with Lucky resting his head on my lap, Denver returned with Otto at his heels. Otto saw Lucky at once and bounded over to us. Lucky stood up to greet Otto, but was only tackled by the smaller dog when he reached him. I laughed when I saw Lucky's look of surprise as Otto tackled him to the ground.

Denver laughed too and when I looked over at him, I saw he had a package in his hands. I was curious, but I didn't say anything until he sat down next to me. He answered my unsaid question by placing the package on my lap and saying, "Here, this is for you. It's a little 'welcome home' gift."

I was startled and stammered, "Y-you didn't have to get me anything, Denver … really."

He shook his head and laughed, "Seriously Zora? Just open the present, will you? Or I'll give it to Otto to rip apart, although I'm not sure the gift will still be in one piece once he's done with it."

"He doesn't look that vicious," I objected, but then as I saw Otto wrestling in the lawn with Lucky, I changed my mind and continued with a sigh, "Fine, I'll open it."

I picked up the present, which was wrapped in thick layers of blue tissue paper, and slowly tore it open. When I saw what it was, I looked at Denver in disbelief and questioned, "How did you know?"

I picked up the green and silver notebook and jet black pen that had my name engraved on it in white as he replied, "I remembered how you were always writing stories in school and just thought you might appreciate having a new notebook and pen to get you started again. I also recall Lucky telling your parents to get you new notebooks and pens, but if they were anything like me, they'll probably think that your last visit was all just a dream. I hope you like it."

I dropped the pen and notebook in my lap and reached over to hug him as I responded, "I love it! Thank you Denver—you're so thoughtful."

We embraced in a warm hug and he kissed my forehead and then stated, "I bet you never got any gifts like this in that crazy land you visited."

"Actually I—" I stopped mid-sentence, suddenly remembering the golden apple and finally realizing that it was missing."

Lucky stopped playing with Otto when he heard the concern in my voice and chuckled, "Sorry Zora, I didn't think you would realize it was missing once you saw Denver in the daylight. I took it from you when the Dove of Light transported you here. It is here, in Denver's yard, and I suppose I will give it back if it will ease your worry."

I didn't reply because I was not sure, but Lucky trotted over to a bush in the yard and retrieved the golden apple from it. Then he came over to me and dropped it in my lap. Denver looked at it at once and when he saw the words inscribed on it, he asked curiously, "What is this for?"

I looked at it as well and replied, "Oh, this is just something one of the guardians gave me. She said if ever his world isn't what it's all made out to be, I can use this to go back to the Land of Inspiration."

"Hmm," he murmured and then he pulled me towards him in a breathtaking kiss, and when he withdrew, the golden apple was in his hands instead of mine. A sly grin was on his face and he said, "You don't need it. I'll hold onto it for you … I'll lock it away so you won't be tempted to go back. You promised you would stay here anyway."

I huffed, but I wasn't angry. At least I knew if he'd ever stop loving me, he'd most likely give the apple back and then I would return to the Land of Inspiration. Denver keeping the apple was like an unspoken promise of love.

We talked then for most of the day, exchanging stories of the worlds we were living in when I was gone for those eight years. He told me of fellow classmates in school and what they've been up to since the last time he's talked to them. Some people he hadn't seen since graduation and others he's seen just a few weeks ago. As he said each of their names, I remembered their faces, and some of these people brought back good memories and others not so much.

Then I told him about the beauty of the Land of Inspiration and all the different guardians I had met there and how they came to be. He stopped me when I told him about Silvershoes, and he asked, in a little disbelief, "A mountain goat? I've got a mountain goat watching over me?"

I nodded and replied, "Hey, whether you like it or not, that's the form you gave the guardian that protects your imagination and leads you in the right direction."

He laughed, "Whatever—I probably didn't even know what a mountain goat looked like when I 'created' him. How is it possible? And how come I don't remember him?"

I shrugged and answered, "You probably don't remember him because you're ashamed to admit you had an imaginary friend, and you probably didn't create him until you saw a mountain goat, maybe his form before was uncertain. The last time you actually *saw* him was when he was a mountain goat. At least that's what I think, but I don't know, it's all very confusing—this guardian stuff—there's probably much more that I haven't even learned about the land."

When the sun started to sink, I realized we had been talking for a long time, and Lucky was still playing in the grass with Otto. Maybe he wouldn't have to leave after all. There was silence while I pondered this, until Denver asked, "Zora? Are you hungry or thirsty? I usually have dinner at this time, and I was hoping you'd join me."

Before I could reply, Lucky stood up and said, "Of course we'd love to join you, but afterwards, if it's not a problem that is, Zora must return to her parents. We don't want them to worry."

Denver stood up and as he pulled me to my feet, he responded, "Of course, I can drop her off afterwards."

Lucky smiled and he and Otto followed me and Denver into the house. In the kitchen, I sat down at the table and Denver asked, "Do you have any preferences? I don't have much of a selection, and the food probably won't taste as good as the stuff you've been eating in the Land of Inspiration, but I—"

I interrupted him with a laugh, "Whatever's easiest for you to make. I'm not a picky eater, Denver, even if I have been spoiled in the Land of Inspiration."

He smiled and I could tell he was relieved. He stated, "All right, it'll be chicken noodle soup then."

He opened up a can of chicken noodle soup and poured it into a pan and then put it on the stove and turned the stove on. As he waited for the soup to heat up he put two bowls and two spoons on the table. Then he asked, "What would you like to drink? I'd offer you wine, but you claim you're still only eighteen, so ..."

I looked up at him and saw a flicker of mischief in his eyes. I shook my head amusingly and replied, "I wouldn't accept it even if I were of age. My memory is coming back and I remember seeing the affects of alcohol at weddings and parties. Besides, you have to take me back to my parents tonight. I know you think I could just stay and then you could take me back whenever and then claim I just came back the day you drop me off, but Lucky wouldn't let you."

He was quiet for a while and he went over to the stove to stir the soup and then he sighed, "You're right ... I'm sorry. So ... milk, juice, pop, water? Any of those interest you?"

"Water's fine, thank you."

He turned back to look at me and questioned, "Water, really? How boring, but I suppose ..."

He opened a cupboard and pulled out two glasses as I said teasingly, "Fine, how about juice then? We can pretend we're two little kids having a tea party."

He smiled and said, "That's a little better. You like apple juice?"

I nodded and replied, "It's one of my favorites actually."

He went over to the fridge and opened it and took out a bottle of apple juice. Then he poured it in our glasses and then returned the bottle to the fridge. I heard a clock ticking, and I spotted one on the wall. I looked at the time as Denver brought over the soup. It was 7:00. As Denver evenly divided the soup between us, he asked, "You're still worrying about the time, Zora? I thought you were here to stay ... unless now it's only daytime visits."

I shook my head and replied, "No. I'm here to stay, I just ... I don't know. Time passes so quickly."

"So then don't waste time looking at the clock. At least that's what I've been told. The clock's going to keep going ... time is going to pass here in this world whether you like it or not. You're going to age now ... I hope you'll be able to handle it."

I grinned, "If you can I can. You're eight years ahead of me."

There was silence then as we ate our dinner, and then we talked some more until Lucky yawned and said, "I hate to be the bearer of bad news, but I am Zora's guardian, and it's time for her to return to her parents' house." Lucky hesitated before he continued, "And Denver. I think it would be wise if this time you just dropped her off and then left before her parents see you, if you catch my drift. The last time she visited she left with you, and she's been gone for a month. If her parents see you again with her, they'll wonder if she actually was in the Land of Inspiration. I can only convince them of so much."

Denver was quiet for a while, but then he agreed, "I suppose you're right." He turned to me then and asked, "I don't suppose you still remember your home phone number do you?"

Before I could tell him I couldn't remember, Lucky rattled off a sequence of numbers and Denver quickly wrote it down. I looked at Lucky and asked, "How do you know what our phone number was?"

Lucky grinned and replied, "It wasn't me who lost my memory." I rolled my eyes and Lucky went on, "Well, let's not let anymore time pass. We must get going."

I sighed heavily, not wanting to leave, and I could tell Denver felt the same way. He retrieved the keys without hurry, and after he had locked Otto in the house, we trudged slowly to the car, with Lucky in the lead. We drove to my parents' house in silence. Lucky made Denver stop on the side of the road to lessen the chance of Denver being seen.

I unbuckled and then opened the car door and Lucky jumped out right away, but I hesitated. I looked at Denver and said, "I had a good time tonight. I'll see you again soon?"

He pulled me towards him and kissed me gently on the lips and then pulled away and replied, "Of course. I believed I would see you again, so now you have to trust me. Okay?"

I nodded and then stepped out of the car, but before I closed the door, Denver said gently, "Zora, I need to hear your voice. Please don't go quiet on me again. Do you trust me?"

He wore a hopeful smile on his face and I returned the smile and said with assurance, "I trust you. Goodnight Denver … I'll see you soon."

Just before I closed the door, I heard him say, "Goodnight Zora. Sleep well."

I walked around the front of the car and follow Lucky towards the house. When I got to the back door and opened it, Denver drove away. I was a little sad to see him leave, but I knew I would be seeing him sometime soon.

Surprisingly the door was unlocked, but when I stepped inside, it wasn't me who talked first. As soon as I closed the door behind me, Lucky began barking, and Mom and Dad rushed into the kitchen. As soon as they saw me, they hurried over and threw their arms around me in a big hug and Mom exclaimed, "I knew it wasn't a dream! I knew you would come back! Oh Zora we missed you! Are you really here to stay now?"

I nodded, but I didn't feel like telling them all about the Land of Inspiration right then. I was suddenly very tired. I yawned and said, "I'm sorry Mom and Dad, but I really want to sleep right now. I'll tell you all about the Land of Inspiration tomorrow if you would like, but right now, I just want to go to bed. I'm exhausted."

Mom and Dad nodded, and Mom said, "Of course, honey. You must've been through a lot. We'll catch up in the morning. Do you still remember where your room is?"

I walked towards the stairs leading to the second floor and replied, "Yeah, I can find my way. Goodnight Mom and Dad. I'll see you in the morning. I love you both."

As they both said their "I love yous" I suddenly wondered why they hadn't said anything about Lucky. At first I thought maybe they hadn't seen him, but that couldn't be it because he was leading me up the stairs and into my old bedroom. I came to the conclusion that they knew I was really tired and were just going to talk to me about it in the morning.

I turned the light on in my room and saw only a bed and the bookshelves crammed with books. I recalled having a dresser and paintings in my room as well, but they must've been moved after I disappeared. It saddened me to see it so empty, but I could tell that the bed sheets were new, and so I knew that Mom and Dad had been preparing for my return somewhat.

I lay on my bed and then turned off the light, but there was still a little daylight outside so that I could see Lucky curl up on the floor next to my bed. He rested his head on his paws, but his eyes were wide and alert. Just as I was about to close my eyes, he jumped up on my bed and whispered gently, "Zora … I know Denver and your parents will take good care of you, and so it is time for me to leave."

I quickly sat up and stammered, "But Lucky, I—"

He cut me off soothingly, "Now Zora, I've told you a million times before that this day would come, and besides I'll always be with you, only … not in this form. It takes too much energy and concentration to keep me like this."

I was scared when he started to glow and I began to cry out, "No Lucky!" But he silenced me again and said more sternly, "No … I can't stay. The Land of Inspiration is calling me. I'll always love you Zora, but it's time for you to finish your life. Please try to understand. I have to disappear because life will become too hectic for you to keep me here as a talking dog, but I will always be protecting your imagination, and so long as you exercise your mind daily, you won't ever lose your creativity. Don't forget me and you'll be okay, but that doesn't mean I'm asking you to mourn over my disappearance. Your mom and dad wouldn't like that, and neither would Denver. Just don't ever deny that you had an imaginary friend like me and I'll be happy."

Tears streamed down my face, but I knew he was leaving me for the best, and so I hugged him and murmured, "Okay then. Goodbye Lucky … we've had a good time together … at least for the most part."

He licked my tears away and scolded tenderly, "Now, now Zora, I won't be having any tears from you right before I leave. We have had a good time and I will continue to watch the many more adventures you will have here on Earth with the people you belong with. Goodbye little one; I'll always love you, and I'll always be protecting you."

I hugged him tightly and then he pulled away softly. He licked me one last time and whispered one last goodbye and then he vanished in a shower of golden light. My room was empty then—his presence being gone and I wanted to cry again, but I felt him brushing against my conscience, ever so slightly, and I was comforted. I lay back down and closed my eyes and made a silent promise to Lucky that I would never forget him and that I would live my life to the fullest and without regrets. I promised him I wouldn't dwell on his absence, because I knew he wouldn't like it. I felt his contentment on my mind and I was soothed and fell asleep.

Chapter 12

Zora

I woke up to birds chirping outside my window. The sound was soothing and it almost reminded me of the birds singing back at the Land of Inspiration. I sat up in my bed and rubbed the sleep out of my eyes. Then I stretched and noticed the smell of chocolate chip pancakes.

I walked downstairs and said good morning to my parents. They hugged me right away as if they were still in disbelief about me being back.

Dad went back over to the stove to flip the pancakes. I sat down at the table and Mom sat across from me and said, "I don't mean to rush things, dear, but I'm really curious about this land you were in. How was it? Did the … were the guardians friendly?"

I nodded and answered, "Oh yes, they were all very kind to me. I was their queen … although I never really did much ruling. Some of the creatures were ordinary animals that you can see around here on Earth and others were quite bizarre. Like there was this white dinosaur creature with black stripes, and he had a jaw disorder so that his bottom teeth stuck over his upper lip and he drooled all of the time. But he was very wise and he helped explain to the other guardians why I should go home."

Mom looked at me in amazement and Dad laughed, "Sounds like you have a lot of stories to tell. We won't have you tell them all in one day though; we don't want to wear you out."

I smiled as Dad put some pancakes on Mom's and my plate. I put some syrup on and as I put a piece of pancake in my mouth, Mom asked, "So where's Lucky this morning then? I saw him last night."

I froze and then swallowed hard. I kept back the tears, but I looked down and my voice was low when I replied, "Oh … he … he had to go. Guardians can't stay here that long in that form. He's still protecting me, but he's protecting me from inside my conscience. He's the only guardian that I know of who other people could actually see besides their creator. It's kind of complicated to explain. All I can say is he lives in the Land of Inspiration where all dreams seem to come true."

Mom reached across the table and put her hand under my chin and tilted my head up so that I had to look at her. Then she said, "I'm sorry Zora, but I'm sure he left for the best. I can't tell you that you'll adjust to this place easily, because I'm not sure what the Land of Inspiration was like, but I can tell you that there are people here that love you as much as those guardians. I love you and dad loves you and so does Bradley, and—"

I intervened and said, "Okay, okay. I know you all love me. I'm just missing a friend right now, but I'll be fine. Besides, I know he's still with me, even now I can feel him."

I finished my pancake then and as I was about to eat a second, the telephone rang. I jumped at the sound and Mom laughed, "Goodness, Zora! It's only the telephone." She then got up and answered it with a friendly "Hello."

There was a pause and then Mom said, "Yes she is, actually; who is this?"

There was a longer pause, Mom hesitated and then she said, "Okay, just a minute. I'll get her."

Mom then put her hand over the mouth piece and said quietly, "Zora—it's Denver Trievus. He told me Lucky told him last night that you were back. He wants to talk to you." She winked at me with a slight smile on her lips as she handed me the phone.

I felt my cheeks grow hot, but I turned away from Mom so she couldn't see me as I spoke into the phone, "Hello?"

I heard excitement in Denver's voice as he exclaimed, "You really did stay! Congratulations Zora, you're human now! Just kidding—you always were—but anyway, the reason why I called is … well … first of all, are you doing anything this afternoon?"

I scoffed, "What would I be doing? I just got back, only you and my mom and dad know I'm alive." I softened my voice and then continued, "But never mind that, what were you planning?"

I could tell he was smiling when he replied, "Actually I already planned it—a picnic in the park if that's okay with you. And possibly a movie afterward if you're up for it. You don't have to come if you don't want to … I mean if you've had enough of me already."

I protested, "Denver! I—"

He cut me off and said teasingly, "I was only joking, but will you come? I can pick you up at noon."

I glanced at my parents quickly, and said, "Hold on a second."

Before I could converse with my parents however, Denver said quickly, "Zora, if you're about to ask your parents if you can go … well … if they ask if we're going out, you can say yes, because we are … unless you don't want to, I mean …" he trailed off uncertainly.

I laughed and replied, "You're funny when you're awkward. If you're asking me out the answer is yes."

He seemed more confident when he replied, "That's exactly what I'm asking. Thanks for helping me out."

I laughed again and then said, "Okay, hold on a second then."

I put my hand over the mouth piece, turned back towards Mom and asked softly, "Mom, Dad? Denver wants to know if I could go on a picnic with him in the park this afternoon. Is that okay?"

Dad was hesitant, but Mom said, "Of course that'd be fine, you shouldn't have to ask us. I mean, even if you were stuck at eighteen, I know you know how to make the right choices, and I've seen your guardian and I know he is always protecting you. You're practically a grownup anyway and you're a smart girl."

I thanked her, grateful of her trust in me, and then spoke into the phone again, "Denver? It's okay. So I'll see you at noon then?"

He was ecstatic, "Yeah, definitely! I'm glad you can come. Okay, I'll see you then."

Before I said goodbye and hung up, I was startled when he said, "Oh, and Zora? I'm really glad you came back. I missed you, and … and I love you."

I hardly found my voice because I was dumbfounded, but I finally replied, "I love you too. I'll see you soon Denver."

He said goodbye then and I hung up. I sat back down and finished my pancakes, and I noticed that as Mom and Dad ate, they glanced at me from time to time with wonder on their faces.

After breakfast, I talked with Mom and Dad about the Land of Inspiration. I told them about Conrad and his magnificent flying and then I told them of Emily and how she at first refused to let me leave the Land of Inspiration because she was scared I wouldn't adjust and that I would be hurt. I spoke of Lucky and how he was the best guardian and how he denied Emily's worries and then how he never gave up on me even when things looked bleak and impossible.

Then they told me how Bradley was doing and how much he missed me. I promised them I would call him after the picnic. It was 11:50 by the time we tired of talking. As I waited for Denver, Mom said excitedly, "When you get home we can go shopping for some new clothes."

"That sounds like fun," I replied cheerfully.

There was a pause, and then Mom added, "But don't feel rushed— enjoy your time with Denver. We can always go tomorrow morning too if you'd like."

I laughed, "Don't worry, Mom. I'm capable of spending time with both of you … I'll be home by seven at the latest."

Denver pulled in the driveway at 12:00 on the dot and I kissed Mom and Dad on the cheek and then hurried towards the door. Before I went out, Dad said, "Have fun, but make the right choices."

I smiled reassuringly at him and then headed out the door. I waved to Denver who was standing at the passenger's side with a wide smile on his face. He kissed me on the lips when I got there and then he opened the door for me. As he walked over to the driver's side, I couldn't help but wonder about the path on Earth I was now traveling, but so long as Denver was with me, I was sure I would be absolutely, one hundred percent okay.

As we pulled out of the driveway and headed towards the park, I felt Lucky brush against my conscience, and he whispered contentedly, "Well done, little one."